COWBOYS
NORTH AND SOUTH

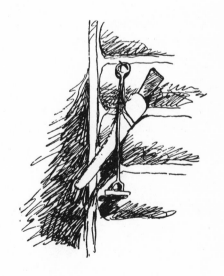

There never was a man what couldn't be throwed –
or a horse what couldn't be rode.

COWBOYS
NORTH AND SOUTH

— *By* —

WILL JAMES

ILLUSTRATED BY THE AUTHOR

TUMBLEWEED
· SERIES ·

MOUNTAIN PRESS PUBLISHING COMPANY
MISSOULA, MONTANA — 1995

Third Printing, June 1996

Library of Congress Cataloging-in-Publication-Data

James, Will, 1892–1942.
    Cowboys north and south / by Will James ; illustrated by the author.
        p.   cm. — (Tumbleweed series)
    ISBN 0-87842-321-4 (pbk. : alk. paper) — ISBN 0-87842-320-6
(hardcover : alk. paper)
    1. Cowboys—West (U.S.) 2. Ranch life—West (U.S.) 3. West (U.S.)—
History—1890-1945. I. Title. II. Series.
F596.J28   1995   95-1853
978'.02—dc20   CIP

Printed in the U.S.A. on acid-free recycled paper.

Mountain Press Publishing Company
P.O. Box 2399 • 1301 S. Third St. W.
Missoula, Montana 59806

PUBLISHER'S NOTE

Will James's books represent an American treasure. His writings and drawings introduced generations of captivated readers to the lifestyle and spirit of the American cowboy and the West. Following James's death in 1942, the reputation of this remarkable artist and writer languished, and nearly all of his twenty-four books went out of print. But in recent years, interest in James's work has surged, due in part to the publication of several biographies and film documentaries, public exhibitions of James's art, and the formation of the Will James Society.

Now, in conjunction with the Will James Art Company of Billings, Montana, Mountain Press Publishing Company is reprinting each of Will James's classic books in handsome cloth and paperback editions. The new editions contain all the original artwork and text, feature an attractive new design, and are printed on acid-free paper to ensure many years of reading pleasure. They will be republished in the order of original publication under the name the Tumbleweed Series.

The republication of Will James's books would not have been possible without the help and support of the many fans of Will James. Because all James's books and artwork remain under copyright protection, the Will James Art Company has been instrumental in providing the necessary permissions and furnishing artwork. Special care has been taken to keep each volume in the Tumbleweed Series faithful to the original vision of Will James.

Mountain Press is pleased to make Will James's books available again. Read and enjoy!

The Will James Society was formed in 1992 as a nonprofit organization dedicated to preserving the memory and works of Will James. The society is one of the primary catalysts behind a growing interest in not only Will James and his work, but also the life and heritage of the working cowboy. For more information on the society, contact:

Will James Society, P.O. Box 8207, Roswell, NM 88202

BOOKS BY WILL JAMES

Cowboys North and South, 1924

The Drifting Cowboy, 1925

Smoky, the Cowhorse, 1926

Cow Country, 1927

Sand, 1929

Lone Cowboy, 1930

Sun Up, 1931

Big-Enough, 1931

Uncle Bill, 1932

All in the Day's Riding, 1933

The Three Mustangers, 1933

Home Ranch, 1935

Young Cowboy, 1935

In the Saddle with Uncle Bill, 1935

Scorpion, 1936

Cowboy in the Making, 1937

Flint Spears, 1938

Look-See with Uncle Bill, 1938

The Will James Cowboy Book, 1938

The Dark Horse, 1939

Horses I Have Known, 1940

My First Horse, 1940

The American Cowboy, 1942

Will James' Book of Cowboy Stories, 1951

PREFACE

What I've wrote in this book is without the help of the dictionary or any course in story writing. I didn't want to dilude what I had to say with a lot of imported words that I couldn't of handled. Good english is all right, but when I want to say *something* I believe in hitting straight to the point without fishing for decorated language.

Me, never being to school and having to pick up what I know in grammar from old magazines and saddle catalogs scattered in cow camps would find plenty of territory for improvement in the literary range, but as the editors and publishers seem to like my efforts the way

I put 'em out, which is natural and undiluded, and being that them same editors and publishers make a successful practice of putting out work that'll suit the readers makes me feel confident enough to give my pen full swing without picking up the slack.

I was born and raised in the cow country, I am a cowboy, and what's put down in these pages *is not material that I've hunted up*, it's what I've lived, seen, and went thru before I ever had any idea that my writing and sketches would ever appear before the public.

For years I've felt the confidence that I could ride and scratch any horse I ever saw. That was a great feeling while it lasted, but too many rough ones gradually shook that confidence out of me, and come a time when I was told that after six months' rest I could maybe ride gentle stock without much danger. I'd rode for the biggest cow and horse outfits from Mexico to Canada, wherever I went I was on a horse, even in the army, and when I was put in the discard to ride only gentle horses was when I tried my hand at drawing and writing of the things I've lived as they really are, and it done me a lot of good to see that my work was accepted by the publishers, not so much for what it brought me as for the chance it gave me to show the readers that a cowboy is just as human as any human ever was and how he's been misrepresented by authors who hunted up material by going thru the country on a Pullman, afraid to mix in the dust and get the true facts.

But it's just as well they didn't, for the cowboy's life can't be learnt in a day or even a year, it's a life you got to be raised at to understand, and I've had it proved that in my work even tho it may be rough, all the folks of the cow countries are backing me in what I say, and I hear the same holler as I used to when riding the side-winding bucker "stay a long time cowboy."

Will James

III

CONTENTS

ILLUSTRATIONS

The rider of them States rides straight up from his head
down to his feet.
~ page 17 ~

The Montana boy might ride his bucker a little looser, but he's
scratching him every jump.
~ page 21 ~

What the cowboy wants is a head-fighting, limber-back cross
between greased lightning and where it hits.
~ page 29 ~

And scratch both ways from the cinch, as the judges may direct.
~ page 30 ~

If the cougar's aim was good, he'd break the mustang's neck
'most as quick as he lit.
~ page 33 ~

The "lobo" wolf was another to help develop "nerves" under the
mustang's hide. He worked from the ground up, and got the
pony to use his front and hind feet mighty well. The teeth
came in handy, too.
~ page 34 ~

And when the cow-puncher's loop spreads over the mustang's
head and draws up, he's fighting the same as he would with
the cougar, he's a bucking, striking, kicking, and biting hunk
of horse-flesh.
~ page 36 ~

And to-day when the bronco-buster takes his rope into the breaking
pen, he finds the Comet strain is still there, some.
~ page 38 ~

He'll make his cowboy shake hands with Saint Peter, and
won't worry whether the ground is under or on the side
of him when he hits.

How many of 'em would like to see the country as it was?

Jim, he'd come up trail into Montana at the "point" of Texas'
first herds.

Jim couldn't follow the old trails much more.

The cowboy was still batting the sheep-herder over the ear with
the six-gun every chance he got.

The freighter would take the nester, his lumber and grub and set
'em way out on the prairie.

I've packed many a hunk of beef for the nester with plenty of
family and no grub.

There's still a country where I can spread my loop without
getting it caught in a fence-post.

The little old three-legged coyote is follerin'.

"Tailing up" is mighty hard, and the critter is never grateful.
~ page 101 ~

I can see by the signs in the snow where she'd stopped and made
a stand.
~ page 109 ~

My horse don't quite agree to all the load and specially
objects to wolves.
~ page 111 ~

It wasn't but a few days when the cattle all knowed what them
V-shaped logs dragging along meant.
~ page 114 ~

One of them ropes sneaks up and snares him by the front feet
just when he's making a grand rush to get away from it.
~ page 121 ~

I gave him a good half-hour to think it over.
~ page 126 ~

Two more such outfits was to start out soon for other directions
and on other ranges.
~ page 131 ~

All that could be got of him was buck, fight, sulk, and
stampede.
~ page 137 ~

After he put a couple of boys in the hospital and come damn
near getting me, he was put in the "rough-string."
~ page 138 ~

*That little horse without man or bridle puts 'er out of the
herd, and heads 'er for the cut.*
~ page 140 ~

*I'd take my rope down and try my luck but that critter would
leave me as though I was standing still.*
~ page 148 ~

*It was a big spotted bull, the kind what wouldn't let a small
object like a horse and a man keep him from going
straight ahead to where he was headed, and I happened
to be in his way.*
~ page 154 ~

*That ornery critter will find his head brought up right
alongside his hind quarters.*
~ page 159 ~

*The first few that are cut out from the main herd for that
"cut" sometimes couldn't be held in one spot, and they
would have to be roped and tied down.*
~ page 161 ~

*Amongst 'em would be a full-grown, long, and lanky steer
with horns of the kind that could more than meet an
argument with most anything.*
~ page 165 ~

*If a lone cow was making a losing fight trying to protect her
calf, all she had to do was let out a call and there'd be
a herd of big steers answering it.*
~ page 167 ~

*For two miles in depth, one right behind the other, come the wild
ones.*

~ page 177 ~

*My saddle was jerked off my horse and I went sailing with it to
Mother Earth.*

~ page 180 ~

I took first turn and sashayed him for a good fifteen miles.

~ page 181 ~

*The wild horse is always ready to go a long way, spring, summer,
fall, or winter.*

~ page 186 ~

Chapter I

COWBOYS NORTH AND SOUTH

I t was early one fall when I plans to hit out for new territory. I'd rode for most of the big outfits north of the Wyoming line up into Canada through Saskatchewan and Alberta. The snow'd come earlier than usual and covered our tarps [short for tarpaulin] and saddles many a time, putting kinks in the ponies' backs to boot, and crimping the old cow horses with rheumatics.

Our ropes, latigos, and saddle blankets were stiff and froze; the wind blowed steady and mud and slush was up to our necks. And the boys from the lower country to the south was bellering at the weather and wishing they was back in the yucca country again, where the sun shined, they said, and lizards was out all winter.

I'd dug up all the clothes I had in my "war bag" and been wearing 'em trying to keep warm, but the rough weather overtook us when we wasn't looking and wasn't prepared for it; consequences is, we rode and froze all day and some more of it on night guard. I'd never been south, but all the decorations the southern hands had to furnish for them paradise valleys by the border kinda unsettled me, and I wanted to drift.

In another month the round-up wagon pulls in and the rumuda turned loose; the superintendent hands us our company checks, telling us to be sure and show up again in time for the spring works.

But, I agrees with some of the boys that I wasn't going to spend my summer's wages buying winter clothes, so, when we got to the railroad six of us buys tickets for as far as Ogden in Utah where we figger to stop for a spell, have a little fun, and proceed south after we got through.

We did have a little fun all right, but after a few days there was only a five-dollar gold piece between all of us. That we used to settle down to business on, and think what we was going to do.

By noon a few of the boys had signed papers and took a job with some cow outfit what was running big in Argentina and wanted American riders for "major-domos," but the old U. S. was good enough for me, and seeing that I wouldn't be no hand at getting out on freight, I wishes the rest of the boys good luck and hits out on my own hook, looking for some way of earning enough dinero to take me to that promised land, the border country.

I'm hoofing it along on one of the main streets of town when I sees one of my breed, head and hat sticking up above the crowd; there's no time lost in getting acquainted and he tells me soon enough that he's on his way to Nevada, to run mustangs.

His brother is there waiting for him with a string of good saddle-horses, he tells me, and if I'd like to come along he'd be glad to have me for my share of the wild ones as wages. That suited me just fine, so he buys two tickets and we leave that night.

The next day when we get off the train and meets the brother, we learn he'd went and got married sudden, and sold all his horses. That leaves us out in the cold, but I still had my old saddle and I was in a stock country.

I finds all the riding I want and it ain't long before I have a string and a steady winter job. But somehow or other I didn't make a very good impression there, and I learns a lot about the reason why as I stay on (it was a couple of years later before I saw the border country).

It seems like Nevada in them days was the hiding-place for a few Montana and Wyoming horse thieves and cattle rustlers; they was good hands with the rope and bronc and shooting iron, they'd get jobs from the big cow outfits, and when a strange rider showed up on the sky-line, it was took for granted by them that hombre was a sheriff, and nary a cow-hand could be seen around camp, for they'd be most all riding down a wash, out of sight and away from it.

It was on account of them few outlaws what found the north too crowded, and hit for some parts of the California Spanish cow countries, that any man riding a double-rigged saddle with the short hard-twist rope tied hard and fast (and not at all like the native of them countries used) was suspicioned to be either a horse thief or cattle rustler, or maybe a stock detective, being his outfit showed he was from other parts.

Like one time I drifted into such a country riding a fine big fat gelding, had a 30-30 carbine under my rosadero and a six-gun in my belt. I was just taking them along, not because I'd need 'em, but just that I wanted to keep 'em.

And I rides into a ranch with my suspicious double-rigged saddle, hard-twist rope, guns, and all, and inquires if I could put up for the night. They're all nice as pie and I'm the same.

The next morning I asks the owner of the place if I could stay on for a couple of days and let my horse rest up, telling him I'd either pay or else start a couple of broncs for him for his trouble, and I buys a little grain to keep my horse in the good shape he already was.

A young feller from up Montana what'd took a little place adjoining this ranch rides in just as I'm saddling a colt what'd been brung in for me. We talks a while and he's sizing me up as we go; then proceeds to tell me how this hombre where I'm staying is spreading around to the neighbors far and wide that from my rigging and actions I'm either a horse thief or a stock detective, which neither is very pleasant to have advertised.

Where he'd got his suspicions was, that I wanted to rest my horse when, to his way of thinking, he didn't need none; besides it was how I'd asked for grain to keep my horse in good shape, and, with the carbine and six-gun all throwed along with the *Miles City* rigging, was enough proof to his judgment that I was something worth watching.

That leaves me in a fine fix, for supposing somebody did steal a bunch of stock anywheres around, why I'd be the goat sure; so when that old gadder rides in that evening I'm waiting for him and reads him the riot for fair. I tells him as to how white men must be darn scarce in this part of the country when he can't recognize one as he sees him riding down the trail (meaning me), and after I get through with him he apologizes a plenty.

But that don't do no good, for when the next day I'm riding away, I stops off the trail to let my horse graze a while (never liked to ride a hungry horse) when looking up through the pines I sees a bunch of men on horseback, and acted like they was following a trail.

I puts two and two together and gets the right conclusion, for when I rides up on the rear of 'em on a high lope I know by the cheap look in their faces that they'd been trailing me to see if I'd took any stock along as I went, and they was disappointed to see me empty-handed.

"You fellers don't know much," I says as a starter, "do you think that if I was a horse thief you'd see me riding along here in daytime, or stopped at that hombre's ranch? No! if I'd been a horse thief you'd never seen me at all and I'd been a thousand miles away from here with the stock before you'd ever got wind of it. Furthermore," I goes on, "if you're all so damn worried as to what I am, look me over and, if you never before seen a man riding a decent rig with a good horse under it, why look again; but I'm just looking for a job and taking my time at it, and I'm not riding for no *one horse* outfit."

But there was just a few spots with folks like that, they meant well but we didn't get the right kind of introduction to 'em, and because a few reckless hombres from the north and east a ways got too free with their ropes, they'd brand everybody what used the same rig they did with the same iron, "N. G."

It seemed like it mattered more what kind of outfit you rode than how good a hand you was; some of 'em didn't like our ways in handling stock and they felt it pretty deep to see better hands with the rope than they was; and that's why I guess I didn't make no hit when I first struck that country, and rode for the first outfit.

I guess the boss remembered one time how he was took down a peg by a little feller from Texas (they used about the same outfit there as we did north). This little feller was riding along with this big overgrown boss; they was roping horses in a pasture and the boss uncoils his sixty-foot rawhide reata, throws it the whole length with

Some of 'em didn't like our ways in handling stock.

a thirty-foot loop, and when it spreads over the horse's neck, with all that rope to spare he ain't got time to take his dallies (turns) around the horn, so he loses his rope. Thirty dollars' worth of rawhide dragging in the dirt.

Now this little feller from Texas was right handy and with his little loop out of a short thirty-five foot "maguay" tied to his saddle horn, he snares the gelding dragging the long reata, picks it up for the boss, hands him the end and tells him quiet and easy: "I'd tie it if I was *you*."

With them kind of goings on and with the different saddle, spurs, bridles, chaps, and ropes, besides the different ways of the folks not saying as to how stock was

9

*This little feller from Texas was right handy and with his short
thirty-five foot "maguay," he snares the gelding.*

handled, all seemed to form a line running north and
south, and dividing the cow country into two separate
territories and ways of doing things; by that, a cowboy
may be a top hand in one State and not be worth much
acrost that line into the other, that is, not till he gets onto
their way of working.

Montana, Wyoming, Colorado, Arizona, New
Mexico, and Texas are, you might say, one territory in
their ways of doing things. The cowboys of them States
are on the move 'most always and get a lot of experience
besides handling broncs and cattle. And I don't ever

remember riding to one of that territory's outfit without somebody said "turn your horse loose and come in"; there was no questions asked as to who you was and nobody was worried. They felt they could take care of you, if you was *good* or *bad*.

From the Mexican border on up to the Canadian line through them States I mentioned you'll find the old pioneers scattered all the way and most of 'em are from Texas; none seemed to've strayed either side much. They took their customs and riggings with 'em and the young cowboy what growed up kept using the same.

The cattle wasn't worked in the corral, everything was done outside on the flats (I'm talking of the big cow outfits). And the reason there's better ropers in them States is because they get more practice, and nothing is done afoot what can be done on horseback.

Oregon, Idaho, California, and Nevada is what you might call the other territory, and acrost the line, they're as true cowmen there as on the east side of that line, only they work different; the cause of it is the country. The big fenced meadows where you got to open ten gates to get a few miles don't call for as many riders, so everything is worked under fence, and when the cattle is turned out on the mountain range, a corral is always hunted up to cut out or brand in. (In this, I'm leaving out the desert countries.)

The rawhide reata is about the only rope, and I seen many a good throw with 'em. I seen 'em handled in ways that was real neat and sure, and I know "dally-men" what never hardly missed getting them dallies going or coming, but never did I see a rawhide man bust his critter and tie it like the boy with the tied whale line could.

There's a lot of danger in a tied rope, and it takes many a twist from the wrist that's not at all simple to do. You got to contend with your horse and the critter at the other end, and the rope what's holding the two together might wind you up if the horse turns, goes to bucking, or gets ornery; and I've seen "wind-ups" that way what'd pretty near cut a rider in two; but the "tie-man," as the boys from Texas on up are called, being they tie their ropes, wouldn't try to take dallies as the Spanish California buckeroo does; for one thing he wants to feel that the critter he piles his rope onto is *his* no matter what happens. What's more he's been raised tying his rope and he can't as a rule get the twist of dallying, and when he gets his fingers pinched, or burned off between the rope and the horn a few times, he's going to stay a tie-man, for he'd rather risk his neck than a hand.

The same with the dally-man of California, Oregon, and Nevada. His rawhide won't stand the strain of being tied; it's got to give and slip some or it'll break. That same rawhide reata ain't even supposed to drag on the ground or be stepped on, for one of the four strands might get a flaw and when it does, it soon breaks at that spot; it's mighty hard for a man using the hard

He wants to feel that the critter he piles his
rope onto is his no matter what happens.

twist to get onto the rawhide. It coils up on him and he can't straighten out his loop, besides he finds it's too much rope, too far to the end.

Then again the Spanish California buckeroo (by that I mean the American cowboy what kept up the early California Spanish style in rig and work) uses a altogether different saddle than the cowboy further east; the horn is higher and wrapped heavy so the turns will grab holt. The rigging is centre fire and the cinch hangs straight down from the middle of the saddle tree. And if you was to tie with them kind of saddles you'd have to pick on a horse with a special good back, and withers or else find yourself saddle and critter going one way and your horse another.

Them saddles answer the purpose of what they're used for, but they'd be no good to a Wyoming hand, cause he'd have to work different on 'em both in roping and riding. The buckeroo of them centre fire countries on riding a bucker or any mean horse sets back pretty well and sticks his feet ahead with stirrup leathers what are set that way. They're a good saddle to ride a mean horse, being there's some jolt it gets you away from; it rocks more and the cantle don't come up and hit you like the double ring would on a kinky back. That's why the contest riders use the centre fire 'most always in the rodeos.

The range rider of Montana, on down to Texas, rides the double cinch, but in the last years the three-quarter rig's been used a lot; in the three-quarter the

*The buckeroo of them centre fire countries sets back pretty
well in his rig and keeps his stirrups ahead.*

cinch sets further ahead than the centre fire, which puts the saddle further back and where it belongs but not as far back as the double rig. The tie rope won't very often yank 'em off, the horn is low and small, not at all fit to take dallies on. With a hard horse they work pretty fair, but not as good as the centre. The rider of them States rides straight up from his head down to his feet, but kinda apt to lean a little forward when the horse is bucking, the riding is some looser but there's a lot of scratching done, and when the old pony quits bucking he'll most likely think there was a couple of wildcats tied by the tail and throwed over his rump.

And when it comes to the bits, there's a big difference again; the spade bit what's used by the dally and centre fire man is a contraption what the Wyoming boys called the "stomach pump" on account of a piece of flat steel what curves a little and goes up the horse's mouth. It's supposed to keep a horse where he belongs, but I find in all the men what's using them bits there's only one out of twenty what knows how. There's a lot in handling them and a good man with the spade bit can work 'most any horse fine. The main secret of it is not to forget it's a "spade" and ought to be handled according, which is light on the rein. Any other way would make a good horse fight his head and worry, and if he starts getting peeved the spade bit is not good; he'll do what he pleases anyway.

In Arizona, to the north and south, the "grazing bit" (as the centre fire buckeroo calls it) is used. It's just a small bit with a curb in the mouth-piece and with very

The rider of them States rides straight up
from his head down to his feet.

little silver on it; laced to the bit is along pair of open reins what are dropped to the ground (if the horse is gentle enough) when the rider gets off.

The buckeroo "across the line" has rawhide reins, not split; to the end of the rein hangs a quirt called a "romal," the head stall is light and all neat with pure silver conchas; whereas the cowboy of Montana on down is apt to use a heavy split ear headstall, and plain.

Then comes the difference in breaking horses. The centre fire man starts his broncs with a hackamore, then maybe a snaffle bit, and back to the hackamore and spade bit both, using double reins, but just letting the colt pack the bit for a spell. When the hackamore is took off, the horse is called a bridle horse. It takes about a year to make him such.

In the tall grass countries on the plains, which is the tie-man's and double-rig country, the broncs are broke mostly with a snaffle — sometimes a loose hackamore with "feador." Soon as he's some bridle-wise the light one-piece curb bit is put on, and his work is with cattle. That's where he learns to be a cow horse and every one of them broncs gets a chance at it.

And I've never seen no better or as big average of real cow horses as the plains and Bad Land countries's got. They get more cow work, where in some countries what used corrals a lot they're just tied up after the cattle is put in, and just a couple of ponies are being used.

Starting west of the Utah line, 'most all riding is done from camps, and very seldom is there a change of horses in one day. There's no night guard, only maybe three or four nights a year, and that's when the cattle is took to the railroad. Sometimes one horse is rode steady for three or four days at a time; and a rule of that country, which is the Spanish California style, and cheats many a buckeroo from practice with the rope, is that the boss takes it to hand to rope all the boys' horses for 'em. The rider comes up with only a hackamore or bridle and takes his horse to saddle (I could never get used to that). The same with working a herd; only a couple of the top hands can take their rope down, but the rest of the boys sure used to make up for it when the boss was away.

In Wyoming or Montana there's no mares allowed in the remuda (saddle horse bunch) while in Nevada or Oregon they use them for leaders, they're called "bell mares" and keep the saddle horses together by just being present. The cause of the difference in them two ways of handling saddle stock is that in one territory a "nighthawk" (night wrangler) is with them herds all night, while in the other they're let loose in little bunches and the bell mare keeps 'em around. (Sometimes.)

It's queer, you'd think — all the different ways of doing things when all the folks are in the same line of business that way; and it struck me the same when I first felt the change a long time ago, but I worked and stayed on all through them countries, drifted south, east, then back north and west again, and while drifting I finds that the early settlers of the different territories are responsible. They blazed the trails and run their cattle to their best way of thinking and each country called for different ways. Neither can be improved much, only maybe with ways that are scientific, but I guess that won't work much on open range; being the cattle is too numerous to be put down by name such as "Bossy" and "Spot," or fed careful and regular like the thoroughbreds.

The stock is all worked and handled to the best advantage and every care is took to get the best out of 'em; there's got to be branding and roping, and it don't matter so much how it's done so long as it's well done.

But there's a steady contest going on in the cow countries, each in their own rig and ways trying to outdo the other, it's with no hard feelings, and each as a rule is willing to credit the other for what he does. Like, for instance, the Montana boy might ride his bucker a little looser, but he's scratching him every jump; whereas, the other from Nevada may be setting close and kinda easy, but not working his legs much. The same with roping — the California boy can handle the reata and take his dallies in fine style, but the Wyoming roper will get his critter down and tied first.

And after you've rode through all these States on both sides of that line I speak of, you'll find that you can tell by the rigging a man's using just what State and pretty near the county the stranger what's just rode in may be from.

A "main herd" in Montana, Wyoming, Arizona, and Texas, goes under the name of "parada" in California, Oregon, and Nevada. A "remuda" changes to "caviada,"

The Montana boy might ride his bucker a little looser,
but he's scratching him every jump.

"slick ear" to "Orejana," "cut horse" to "part horse," "cowboy" to "buckeroo," etc., etc., but it all goes to the same critter and the same things and the same work, only a different way and style to fit the country.

These last years since Texas started putting up windmills and fences for the stock, the cowboy from there drifted north into Wyoming and Montana, where some time later that same daggoned barb wire cut the trails and made riding scarcer.

Then it was about time for the "rannies" to pull up their ponies and figger where to go next. They remembered how they left Texas and how every State from there north was feeling the pinch of the fences. So every year a few was hitting acrost the Rockies and stringing out into the sage-brush territory.

There was a many a time when remembering the old prairie States as they *was* that they'd give both arms to see it that way again, the gray sage didn't wave like the blue joint of the creek bottoms, the little twisted grama grass looked scared comparing with the "prairie wool," and the cattle seemed to be all neck reaching for shadscale and sniffing for water.

But a few years winding around that sage and buck brush on two meals a day, riding the same horse from sun-up till sundown kind of broke 'em in and weaned 'em away from the tall grass countries. There was no guard to be stood and that helped some, and again it was pretty nice to find a solid old cow camp with a dry floor and a roof when the sleet and snow started coming.

Then came a time after them few years when, in that centre fire country, spots was located where fences wasn't to be found, and even though most of the work in branding was done in corrals and the ways of working was changed some, the boy with the tied rope got to liking it near as well as the prairie he was raised into. The big hard pan flats, the deep arroyos with sides of malapi, and the scrub juniper or spooky joshua got to look different and kinda good.

And that's why to-day in that country and riding along with the centre fire and dally man, you'll see the boy with the double or three-quarter rig packing his short whale line and riding both alongside one another.

In the breaking corral, or in bull-dogging, roping, and general range work, you'll see 'em competing against one another, them two riders of the same profession but of different countries and ways.

And you'll find that even though one is always trying to outdo or show the other up, there's no snickering done, instead there's admiration in the skill each one shows in his perticular way, for they was both raised at doing things in that one way of theirs, and if they rode for a hundred years they'd never change them, for in each their way they learned to do something what takes skill, practice, and nerve, and neither can improve.

Chapter II

BUCKING HORSES AND BUCKING-HORSE RIDERS

I n most countries a mean horse is got rid of or broke of his meanness by either kind or rough handling. He may be given away to some enemy or shipped and sold at auction — that ornery devil, dragging all the bad names after him, will keep on drifting and changing of scenery till he's too old to be shipped or traded any more. He's a mighty expensive animal, figgering all the buggies he kicked to pieces, the harnesses he tore up, and the stalls he broke down, not counting injury to them what tried to handle him. But there's a place for such horses.

It's anywheres west of the Laramie Plains. If you've got a real ornery, man-eating, bucking, striking, can't-be-rode animal of that kind, he's sure worth a lot, and if he's worse than that he's worth more.

Fact is, there's people out looking for them kind of ponies, and they'll give from a hundred on up for 'em.

They're the hombres who's responsible for these "Frontier Day Celebrations," "Rodeos," "War-Bonnets," "Reunion," and "Round-ups," and they must have mean horses, the meaner the better. They must have horses that'll give the boys what's rode in for the events a chance to show what they can do, 'cause if the rider "up" gets a bronc that just crowhops, it don't matter how easy he rides, or how much he fans him, and how loud the crowd in the grand stand cheers and hollers, the judges of who's the best rider won't notice him, being he has nothing hard to stick. That's where a good, hard, mean, bucking horse is wanted, he's got to have enough wickedness in him for that cowboy to work on — I've seen mighty good riders left out of the prize money on account of the horse they drew, just because that pony wasn't mean enough; and that old boy a-setting up there with taped spurs and fighting mad, blood in his eye and a-wishing something would blow up under his bronc so he could show the world and the judges what a wolverene he is on horse-flesh.

Nobody gets credit for riding easy in a rocking-chair. What the cowboy wants is a head-fighting, limber-back cross between greased lightning and where it hits — a horse that'll call for all the endurance, main strength, and equilibrium that cowboy's got — just so he can show his ability and scratch both ways from the cinch, as the judges may direct. There's when a mean devil of a is horse wanted; he gets a chance to show how mean he is with free rein, and the cowboy has something worth while to work at.

*What the cowboy wants is a head-fighting, limber-back cross
between greased lightning and where it hits.*

And scratch both ways from the cinch, as the judges may direct.

I've knowed some great horses in that game — there was Long Tom, Hammerhead, Old Steamboat; that last was a great old pony, eleven hundred pounds of solid steel and action and a square shooter. They say he never was rode, but I know he has been rode to a standstill. They was real riders that did it, tho'. I figgered that horse was part human the way he'd feel out his rider. He'd sometimes try him out on a few easy jumps just to see how he was setting, and when he'd loosen up for the last, it's safe enough to say, when that last would come and the dust cleared, there'd 'most always be a tall lean lanky bow-legged cowboy picking himself up and wondering how many horses he'd seen in the last few seconds. I've seen Old Steamboat throw his man with his head up and four feet on the ground, but what happened before he got in that peaceful position was enough to jar a centipede loose — and a human's only got two legs.

A horse is not trained to buck, as some folks think; out there on the open range he already knows how; sometimes the bronco-buster encourages him at it for either fun or practice for the next Rodeo, and the bronc, as a rule, is more than willing and might keep on bucking every time he's rode whether the rider wants him to or not. Close as I could figure it out, the blame for originating the bucking, striking, and biting in the Western horse goes a heap to the mountain-lion and wolf — them two terrors of the range, mixed with instinct and shook up well with wild, free blood, kinda allows for the range-horse's actions. The bucking was first interduced when that stallion "Comet" got away from the Spaniards with his few mares, years before Texas was fought for; he started a wild bunch that kept multiplying, till all of Old Mexico and the Southern States was a grazing country for his sons, grandsons, and daughters — they are the real mustang — more horses were brought in from Spain, and Comet's sons would increase the little bands by stealing mares from the pastures; some would get away, join whatever bunch they could, and in no time be as wild as the rest.

Them old ponies had a lot to deal with. The mountain-lion was always a-waiting for 'em from his perch, where he could easy spring down on his victim; he'd fall on their necks, grab holt with front claws and teeth, a foot or so from the ears, then swing his hind quarters down with all his strength and clamp his claws under the horse's jaw close to the chin, jerk the pony's head up, and, if the cougar's aim was good, he'd break the mustang's neck 'most as quick as he lit. Once in a while the pony would shake free, but there'd be a story plain to see as to how Mr. Lion worked. The chin was gone and there'd be gashes in the neck that'd leave scars many inches long and plenty deep.

The "lobo" wolf was another to help develop "nerves" under the mustang's hide. He worked from the ground up, and got the pony to use his front and hind feet mighty well. The teeth came in handy, too, so all in all after his enemies got thru edicating him, there was a new nerve took growth and spread from the tip of his ears to the tip of his tail — that nerve (if such you would call it) commanded action whenever anything to the mustang's dislike appeared or let itself be known in any way. And when the cowpuncher's loop spreads over the mustang's head and draws up, he's fighting the same as he would with the cougar, he's a bucking, striking, kicking, and biting hunk of horse-flesh to anything that's close.

The mustang made a mighty fine cow horse and was good enough till, about forty years or so ago, the stockmen started buying blooded horses from the East and Europe to breed up bigger saddle stock. The stallions were mostly French coach and Hambletonians; some registered mares

If the cougar's aim was good, he'd break
the mustang's neck 'most as quick as he lit.

The "lobo" wolf was another to help develop "nerves" under the mustang's hide. He worked from the ground up, and got the pony to use his front and hind feet mighty well. The teeth came in handy, too.

were bought, too — the cross between the hot-bloods and mustangs brought out fine big horses — but, man, how they could buck!

The mustangs kept a-getting chased and caught; they were fence-broken, some "ham-strung," and turned into big pastures where they could range winter and summer, year in year out. In each bunch you could see a thoroughbred, and the herds were showing the blood more every year — but the bucking was still there and worse than ever, the colts never saw a human from the time they were branded till they were four-year-olds, and some never saw one till they were ten. If they did it wasn't for long, a snort, a cloud of dust, and the rider was left behind a ridge, unless that perticular rider had intentions of catching some, and he sure had to be mounted for that.

As a rule, when a bunch of broncs was wanted out of the "stock" horses — there'd be a "parada" (herd of about 100 broke horses) held together by a few riders — the wild ones would be hazed (not drove) toward the "parada," the riders holding the milling herd would hide on the side of their horses and let the wild ones get in — then there'd be a grand entrée fast and furious into the big corrals, and before the broncs knew it they were surrounded by a good solid stockade of cottonwood poles, ten feet high.

The thoroughbred stallion which was so gentle a few years before was as wild as the herd with him, he'd never show any symptoms of ever having seen a human or ever wanting to see one, he'd forgot his warm box stalls and his feeds of grain, the freedom he'd experienced was worth more to him than what man could give him. He was proud of his band, his colts were big and slick even tho' not better or tougher than the mustang already was.

And to-day when the bronco-buster packs his saddle into the breaking pen, takes his rope, and catches his bronc to break, he finds that the Comet strain is still there some — it's blended with the "blue dog" of Texas along with the Steeldust, Coach, Standard Bred, etc., and scatters all thru the Western States, the Canadian prairies, and Mexico. The imported thoroughbred can't kill that

And when the cow-puncher's loop spreads over the mustang's head and draws up, he's fighting the same as he would with the cougar, he's a bucking, striking, kicking, and biting hunk of horse-flesh.

strain; fact is, they make it worse; for, even tho' the pure blood would never buck, the cross forms a kind of reaction, with the result that the foals sure keep up the reputation of the mustang that was, and then some. The freedom of the open range and big pastures the Western horse gets is all he needs, and he'll always be ready to give his rider the shaking up he's expecting.

I wouldn't give "two bits" for a bronc what didn't buck when first rode, 'cause I figgers it's their mettle showing when they do. It's the right spirit at the right time — every horse what bucks is not a outlaw, not by a long shot. I've seen and rode many a good old well-broke cow horse what had to have his buck out in the cold mornings, just to kind of warm hisself up on the subject and settle down for the work ahead.

The outlaw (as some call him) he's the horse that won't quit bucking and fights harder every time he's saddled; it's his nature, and sometimes he's made one by too rough or not rough enough handling, and spoiled either by the bronc peeler what started to break him or else turned loose on the range before he's thoroughly broke, to run for months before he's caught up again. A colt can be spoiled in many ways, and reckless riders what are good riders have spoiled more horses than the poor ones have, 'cause the good rider knows he can ride his horse whatever he does or whichever way he goes, whereas the poorer rider is kinda careful and tries to teach his bronc to be a cow horse; he won't let him buck if he can help it.

There's a difference in horses' nature and very few can be handled alike. Some are kinda nervous and full of life, them kind's got to be handled careful and easy or they'd get to be mean fighters as a rule. Then there's what we call the "jughead"; he's got to be pulled around a heap, and it takes a lot of elbow grease to get him lined out for anything; and there's another that as soon as a feller gets his rope on him makes him feel that either him or the bronc ain't got far to go. He's the kind of horse with a far-away look; some folks call 'em locoed. But whether he's that or not he'll sure take a man thru

And to-day when the bronco-buster takes his rope into the breaking
pen, he finds the Comet strain is still there, some.

some awful places and sometimes only one comes out. Such doings would make a steeplechase as exciting as a fat man's race; that horse is out to get his man and he don't care if he goes himself while doing the getting. He's out to commit suicide and make a killing at the same time. I pulled the saddle off such a horse one time after a good stiff ride; of a sudden he flew past and kicked at me with his two free legs, snapping and biting at the "jakama" (hackamore rope), heading straight for the side of the corral, when he connected with it and fell back dead, with a broken neck. I felt kinda relieved 'cause I knew it was either him or me or both of us had to go; he'd tried it before. There's a lot of them used at the round-ups and rodeos being that they mean business that way — that kind most generally can sure buck and will give a rider a chance to show his skill; but they 'most always wind up a-straddle the grand-stand's fence with a piece of broken timber thru 'em, and the rider is lucky if he comes out with just bumps.

And again there's the horse what keeps his brain a-working for some way to hang his rider's hide on the corral or anywhere it'll hang, and save his own hide doing it. He's crooked any way you take him, and will put so much energy in his bucking that when he's up in the air all twisted up, he don't figure or care about the coming down. He'll make his cowboy shake hands with Saint Peter, and won't worry whether the ground is under or on the side of him when he hits. When he falls, he falls hard, and the rider has little chance to get away. That pony seldom gets hurt, he's wise enough to look out for himself; what's on top of him is what he wants to get rid of, and he won't be on the square trying it.

Out of every hundred buckers of the arena there's only about fifteen that are square and will give a man a fair battle. Old Steamboat was that kind, he was gentle to saddle and handle, but when he felt the rider's weight and the blind was pulled off, it was second nature and fun for him to buck, and he knew as well as the boys did that he could buck.

Horses have a heap more brains than some folks would like to give 'em credit for, and if they want to be mean they know how. The same if they want to be good; the kind of interduction they get with man has a lot to do with it.

Most any bronc is a ticklish proposition to handle when first caught; it's not always meanness, it's fear of the human. They only try to protect themselves. Sometimes by going easy and having patience according, a man can break one to ride without bucking, but even at that, the meanest bucking horse I ever saw was gentle to break, and never made a jump till one day he got away and run with the wild bunch for a couple of years. When caught again, an Indian with the outfit rode him out of camp, with the old pony going "high, wide, and handsome." The Indian stuck, but along about noon he comes back, afoot. It was during fall round-up when that horse was caught once more; his back had been scalded by the saddle and all white hair grew where it had been.

*He'll make his cowboy shake hands with Saint Peter, and won't worry
whether the ground is under or on the side of him when he hits.*

He took a dislike for saddle and men with the result that the next year he was sold to a Rodeo association for the Cowboys Reunion.

To-day there's more buckers like that in the hills waiting to be brought in, buckers as good as Old Steamboat or any of 'em ever was. They're fat and sassy and full of fight, and in them same hills and range there's riders what keeps their eyes on 'em a-figgering to bring 'em in and "buck 'em" for first money when the Rodeo is pulled off. If the association's got harder buckers, them is what they want; for as long as there's fighting broncs, there's going to challenging riders, and in all the cowboys I've met and buckers I've handled and seen on the open ranges or arenas of U. S., Canada, and Mexico, I've still got to see the rider what couldn't be throwed and the horse what couldn't be rode.

Chapter III

A Cowpuncher Speaks

I'm up on a knoll. The river-bottom stretches out below me, and far as I can see is a checkered country of little pastures, fields, and alfalfa patches, fences a-cutting up the land and a-stretching 'way up over the ridges. It all looks so peaceful and I wonder if it's as it looks. I wonder if that man out there working in his field, worrying about his crop or mortgage, appreciates or sees what's about him. There's so many gates, ditches, and bridges, it seems like they're down a hole and sort of trying to get out of the entanglements.

How many of 'em would like to see the country as it was; how many have rode across the river-flats when the neighbor was some fifteen miles or so away? When the only fence was a little "wrango" horse pasture and the big pole corrals? The hills were black with cattle then, more cattle than this country will ever see again; there was a lot of freedom, no mortgages, and you were glad

How many of 'em would like to see the country as it was?

when your neighbor rode in and sat at your table remarking "how good" *his own beef* tasted for a change.

There's old Jim Austin who's got the real-estate office up above the bank — at one time he was paying taxes on fifteen thousand head of cattle (which means he was running closer onto twenty-five thousand of the critters), had a couple thousand horses and twenty thousand acres of land — some of it government land he'd bought for as low as two bits an acre, the rest he got from the homesteaders who'd leave the country and trade their "three hundred and twenty" for a ticket back home. It's the same land I'm looking at now, but you wouldn't know it.

Jim, he'd come up trail into Montana at the "point" of Texas' first herds; the cattle was 'most head, and horns averaging six foot from tip to tip. He was a "top hand" and reckless as they make 'em; had nothing but a string of broncs and good health. He'd traded his wages for cattle, and every fall when the last of the beef was shipped you could see Jim driving his summer's wages home, all good young she-stock he'd bought here and there, along with a few "slicks" he thought *might* be his.

Once in a while he'd get on a rampage and leave all his cattle on the poker-table, but it wasn't long till there'd be another little bunch at the home corrals bearing the Austin "iron," and Jim would make a new promise, till finally a schoolmarm made him keep it — and that was to never touch cards or "likker" again. He got so he wouldn't ride bad horses any more, so interested he was in making a go of what he'd started.

His herds kept increasing and spreading over the government range; his little squatter's right was three hundred and twenty acres and the unsurveyed land about him was same as his. He wasn't crowded for room.

Then out of a clear sky came the smell of sheep; all was O. K. at first, 'cause the cowmen figgered there was plenty of range for everybody, *even sheep*. But soon enough the sheep kept getting thicker and their range poorer, which started the crowding on the cowman's best bits of country. There was a few parleys without the voice of the "smoke wagon" being heard — but sheep and sheep-herders don't have much respect for words or rules or country; so they went at it to start spoiling it all; and the cowmen went on to finishing what the sheepmen had started, with the result that mostly sheepmen and sheep was missing. The government couldn't do much; they'd had to pinch about four States.

The cattlemen won for a spell and all was hunkydory again outside of the damage sheep had done to the range. The dust beds they'd made out of the good grassy "benches" was beginning to show signs of life, the air was pure as ever, and cattle was getting fat. The cattlemen were all good folks once more and tending to their business in the land that was theirs. They were the first to blaze the trail to it; they made that land a big beef-producing country, it was their home, and naturally they wouldn't allow a stinking

Jim, he'd come up trail into Montana at the "point" of Texas' first herds.

sheep coming along and leaving nothing of it but the bad odor.

Jim Austin rode in one day and went on to tell Mrs. Austin what a fine neighbor had just moved in and took a "squatter's" just five miles down the river. A few months later another sets up a tent and starts a shack, up river this time and only two miles away. "Well, that was all right; there's lots of room, but I can't see how they're going to make a go of 'farming,'" Jim said; "this country's too dry." Anyhow, they kept a-coming, and it wasn't long till Jim couldn't follow the old trails much more. He'd bought all the government land he could, but that was nowheres near enough to run even one-fifth of his cattle. His leases couldn't hold the homesteader back, only sheep. Some of his best springs were filed on and taken away from right inside his lease. Then the sheep showed up again; the homesteader wasn't worried about sheep, they couldn't do him no harm, so they were neutral, and the cattlemen went at it again alone. It was a losing fight; their range was being taken from 'em one way or another, and they hadn't much heart to saving what little was left. So they tried it in another way and speculated some. In the meantime their cattle was still eating what little feed the sheep hadn't shoved into the earth, and the cowboys was still swapping a few shots with the sheep-herder and batting him over the ear with the six-gun every chance he got.

The freighters were kept busy hauling out the nester. He'd take them, their lumber, grub, and all, and set 'em 'way out somewhere on the prairie wherever their

Jim couldn't follow the old trails much more.

particular homestead was at. Few of 'em had enough money to buy an outfit like team and wagon, and they went out any way, figuring on buying the next spring; besides, they'd know better what they wanted when they got there. They did all right, but not till the freighter had already left, and then they realized what a big country they were in. The first few had no close neighbors to go to and borrow from. I guess it seemed they was all alone in the whole world.

The booster had most of the folks who'd come West to homestead believing that all was fixed for them out here. All they'd have to do would be to go on and farm a little; the windmill would be a-running for 'em and the

*The cowboy was still batting the sheep-herder over
the ear with the six-gun every chance he got.*

chickens waiting to be fed. Some paradise, and no wonder
they flocked after they heard so much about the climate
being so fine and the soil being so rich! The soil *was* fine,
all right, and the climate was good, but it needed water
to grow what they planted. Well, they planted and waited,
planted and waited in succession for years. The crop would
come up fine in the spring, just fine enough for feed,
then dry up. It was a cow country and should have been
left such; but the nesters kept on hoping and working;
the little money they'd brought with 'em was gone, and
the little homestead was all they had. Some writers would

have it that the stockman hired gunmen to drive the nesters off, but I'm here to say that I've packed many a hunk of beef on the back of my saddle for a certain nester with plenty of family and no grub. While working a herd we'd sometimes break a steer's neck or leg in roping. Jim would 'most always send one of us boys to the nester closest to tell him bring his wagon and scatter this critter among his neighbors.

One winter while riding for weak stock, and thirty miles from camp, I see one of them nester shacks in the distance and getting dark. I figgers on putting up at the place for the night, if satisfactory with the owner. I rides up and the place looks deserted; no tracks on the week-old snow and no smokes out of the pipe or light to be seen. I gets off my horse and knocks. Some one answers inside and there's a note in the voice that suggests lost hopes coming back. Opening the door I sees an old man in his bunk by the corner; had everything over him he could get — horse-blankets, sacks, and old clothes was piled high. It's a wonder he could move, but he did; that is, his head anyway, and tells me to "come in." I finds he has nothing but eight cans of corn between him and starvation. He kept warm by staying in bed or walking around when he could. He'd burnt his last fuel a month ago, even to the shelves, benches, and table he'd made; said he knew if he'd lose sight of the shack he'd get lost — and the bleak prairie outside all white without a break nowheres didn't look very promising to a newcomer — town was seventy miles

*The freighter would take the nester, his lumber
and grub and set 'em way out on the prairie.*

away. He'd had a freighter haul his lumber and grub
for him, figgering to stay on the homestead the
winter and working away in the summer, and that
way get title for the land. But him being a townman
had no idea how much grub a human could eat in
six months' time, and figgered about three months
short. The little tin stove in the corner eats a lot
too, and it was too late to gather "buffalo-chips,"
too much snow over 'em; besides, he'd need a wagon
and team; so he'd et his corn cold.

I rides back that night and gets to the ranch for
breakfast, tells Jim about it, and in a short while
one of the boys is headed for the nester's shack with
a little grub and an extra horse to bring the old
man to the ranch with.

There was many like that; some families even hit the trail for the prairies that way, with all kinds of hopes and little knowing what they had to buck up against. The pioneer stockman who'd lost his country to 'em was man enough to help 'em; he didn't have to hire no gunman. All he'd had to've done was to ignore 'em and would've got rid of many that way. He didn't, cause it wasn't in him. He liked fair play, and even though he didn't get it from some, that's the way he dealt.

Fact is, I know of plenty of times when cattlemen would find some of their cattle or horses shot down. It looked like it was done just for spite and it always struck me kind o' small for anybody to even scores that way. The sheepman wouldn't do it, it wasn't his style. And I remember, before the nesters came in, the latch-string hung out always; but with the nester or what followed him it wasn't safe to be too hospitable and leave the door open. A 30-30 carbine would disappear, or blankets, also saddles and grub; so the padlock was fastened to the cow camp and will stay there as long as there is one.

One spring, a strong warm "chinook" came, and mighty early. It took two feet of snow off the level, and kept on a-blowing hot; took most of the moisture out, and it was too early for the nesters to plant, for fear of the frost that was bound to come. The moisture that fell after that wasn't enough to wet a cigarette paper, and it blowed 'most always. The ground was dry, and

*I've packed many a hunk of beef for the nester
with plenty of family and no grub.*

where it had been ploughed it shifted fine. They didn't plant that year — they was leaving, out of the prairies back to home or anywhere else they could get, just so they got away.

Jim Austin was squatted by the corral counting the ears off the calves branded that day. "Mighty poor calf crop this spring," he thought; "cattle too scattered." He figgered he'd have to cut down the herd some more and run 'em closer to home.

A few days later Jim straddled his "top-horse" and told his wife not to expect him back for a few days. He was gone a week — and on his return he told a "wrango" to corral all the broke work-horses on the ranch, and told the ranch hands to grease up all the wagons and hitch a four-horse team to each. Us cowboys kept a-branding calves but we were sure a-wondering what was up. Finally it was learned that he bought all the homesteads he could get that was *proved on*, and was helping the nesters what hadn't already gone to move their belongings and families to the railroad. They was mighty glad to sell for enough to get back home on, and that way Jim was trying to get his old range back. Though he was sorry for the nesters, he knew there was no use — this was a cow country and always will be.

The nesters' fences was tore down and built up again, but it took in bigger territory. Some places the fence was a solid ten miles long and five wide. It was a winter range, and Jim kept on paying two cents lease an acre for thousands of acres of government land and fenced that in too. Sheep had the rest of the country buffaloed and dying. Some cattlemen still run their stock out on the free range, but they weren't doing good, and the winters left many a bone pile in the coulées.

Riding up the bottom one day, Jim come across a whole outfit of tents, mules, and men in high-laced boots. They were surveyors and engineers looking over the prospects for a dam and irrigation canal. Jim got on his "high horse" right away and was fighting mad. He felt it was a new trap to beat and crowd him out of what he'd built, scraped together, and saved. He was satisfied to be left alone the way things was. The fact that the irrigation system would make his land worth ten times more didn't faze him none. He'd forgot about the colts he'd rode out to bring in and started back to the ranch feeling kind o' tired. There sure didn't seem to be no use fighting any longer; progress wanted his freedom.

The dam was built and Jim helped build it with shares. The canal cut through the old stage roads and trails and left a scar of many colors on the side of the river breaks. Most of his government lease was taken away from him; being it was under the canal and subject to irrigation, the land was sold at high price, and this time the nesters was called "farmers" and came in to stay. There was water and plenty of it; little ditches run through the river-bottom and alfalfa began to grow. Haystacks and a few head of dairy stock were seen here and there. Jim held on and refused to sell any of his land. The range being overcrowded for years was mostly loco and sage-brush and rocks. The stirrup-high "blue joint" was gone. He had to cut down his herd and saw where what he kept would have to be fed in winter. His own land had to be divided up with more fences and ditches, mowers and hay-rakes bought, and Jim tried to get himself used to seeing it all. It sure hurt, but it had to be. His white and brockle-faced stock crowded the fences at first fall. There was no more rustling in 'em, and the hay he'd cut looked better to them than the dry range. Jim didn't wonder; he knew how it was going to end — and it cut pretty deep when his cowpunchers'd rode in with wire pliers fastened to their saddles instead of the good old shootin'-iron at their belts.

The government didn't seem to care or realize that the cattle industry was being killed. They let sheep run in the country that could be ruined, when there was other States what might have been made sheep reserves and where their sharp hoofs could do no harm. They let the booster bring people out on the prairies that couldn't be dry-farmed. The proof is up on the benches. You'll see hundreds of deserted shacks; the land is ploughed around 'em and only weeds is where the buffalo-grass used to grow. What little is under irrigation don't no more than feed the few cattle, hogs, and sheep. Not much goes out — that is not near as much as when it was a cow country. The land is dying and it will die unless it's given a chance and the sheep are took off and put away in the burned lava country.

Some folks would call it a great country, a heap greater they think than it ever was; but it don't seem like the United States any more. Take the little town of Garrison, for instance — it used to be our shipping-point — grew overnight, you might say; new hotels was built to accommodate the pilgrims, and there'd be only one hombre out of four what you might call American. The rest was from 'most everywhere where it was crowded. Two new banks sprang up, and on the second floor of the biggest you could see the gold letters in the big windows saying

JAMES AUSTIN, REAL ESTATE

Yep, Jim had quit, turned all of his cattle he could into beef and shipped to Chicago. The mixed stock was sold at auction; his ranch was divided into small farms, which accounts for the real-estate office. It was for sale. Antonio Spagaroni had bought a hundred acres; he didn't need to hire no help. All the young Spagaronis and the Missus was working. He'd take his best pork and chickens to market and keep for himself what he couldn't get rid of. "Oh! yes, thees fine coontree."

When the armistice was signed the railroad rates went up and the cattle prices went down. The folks in the big cities were paying four prices for beef and the stockmen were losing in shipping; like one told me he'd shipped a car-load of hides and got a bill from the buyer, who said the hides didn't pay for the freight; that he'd have to send another car-load. It was a joke but there was a heap of truth in it. The cowmen were in debt and going under; they had to shift for themselves and were neglected and put back for other governmental needs. Nobody seemed to mind if beef was plumb out of sight in the butcher-shops.

Jim loaned out all he could to help his pioneer friends, at the same time glad he was out of it. There were no corrals or bellering cattle nowheres near him. He'd bought a home in Garrison, and on the walls of the big living-room you can see a few big paintings of Charley Russell's — Montana's cowboy artist. Jim knows every brush-mark on 'em. They represent happenings of the days when the range was free and open. There's no sheep or nesters'

*There's still a country where I can spread my loop
without getting it caught in a fence-post.*

shacks to mar the scenery, and he'll tell you it's mighty good medicine for sore eyes and a tired heart.

He was studying one of them paintings as I walked in, and when he saw me he knew what was up. I'd been with Jim ever since he got enough cattle to hire an extra rider. I was his cow foreman and fought sheepmen with him and tried to help him save his little country. I saw it go under but I stayed to the end. When riding got scarce and he had to let the boys go one by one, me being the only one left, he still kept me on the payroll. Men for the hay-fields was hard to get, but he'd never asked me to get off my horse and ride the mowing-machine. He knew my feelings as a cowpuncher, admired and respected 'em that way. My wages never would work the way Jim's did. I was willing to let 'em go and have a little fun once in a while. I've got a home with him if I want to take it, but I feel like hittin' the breeze some; new scenery is real good sometimes.

There's a scope of country that stretches hundreds of miles north and south of the Santa Fe. The tourists when they go through it pull down their windows for fear of the dust. You can hear 'em say, "What an *awful* country it is; how desolate and destitute of life; a person would surely die of loneliness living in such a dreadful place," etc. Well — that's where I'm headed for, if I don't get my throat cut by barb-wire before I get there. The water-holes are forty miles apart and maybe dry when you get to 'em. You'd be surprised but there's cattle there and no fences. Fact is, the country ain't worth fencing. The only gate is on the corral by the spring. When you get out of it on your crow-hopping bronc you're free to go whichever way you please. The old trails are the same there, and I can spread my loop without getting it caught in a fence-post. It's a place where nesters never stop and sheep can't live.

Some folks call it the country God forgot, but I thinks different.

As I'm setting upon this little knoll taking a last look at the country where I'd put in so many hard rides, a little old coyote ambles up the side of the hill, sees me and stops, starts to run some more, then somehow feels that I'm harmless and stops again. I see him limping and notice a trap kept one of his paws. He, too, has been crowded a heap, and somehow I have more admiration for him than I used to. I'd like to let him know we're not enemies no more.

The sun is going down as I straddle my horse and head south for an all-night ride. It's most dark before I look back. I can see the outline of the river breaks I know so well, and not so far behind I can hear the Yip! Yip! of the little old three-legged coyote — he's follerin'!

The little old three-legged coyote is follerin'.

Chapter IV

CATTLE RUSTLERS

Ragged, bewhiskered, narrow-brained, cruel, and mighty dangerous to all folks, specially women, unscrupulous, with a hankering to kill and destroy all what he runs across, leaving nothing behind but the smoke and a grease spot, is the impression folks get thru the movies and other fiction of the cattle rustler and horse thief.

I don't blame them folks for shivering at the thought of ever meeting such a bad hombre, but they can rest easy, 'cause there is no such animal in the cattle rustler. Picture for yourself a man sleeping out under the stars, watching the sunrise and sunsets, where there's no skyscrapers or smoke to keep him from seeing *it all*, acting that way or being what *they* say he is.

When I speak of cattle rustlers, I don't mean them petty cheap crooks what's read dime novels and tries to get tough, steals some poor old widow's last few "dogies" cause they ain't got guts enough to get theirs from the big outfits what keeps riders the year 'round — them kind don't last long enough to be mentioned anyhow — and I always figgered the rope what kept 'em from touching the earth was worth a heap more than what it was holding.

To my way of thinking anybody with a lot of nerve is never real bad all the way, whether he be a cattle thief, or cattle rustler — the excitement he gets out of it is what he likes most, and you can bet your boots that even tho' he may be dealing from the bottom of the deck, he's taking his from them what won't suffer from the loss, or maybe even miss it; you're plumb safe when that kind rides up to your camp to leave your silver mounted spurs and bits scattered around as usual, and most likely if he sees you're in need of a fresh horse he'll be real liberal in offering you the pick of his string — only danger is, if you're caught riding one of them ponies, it may be kind of hard to explain just how you come in possession of said animal.

There's cases where some cowboy what's kind of reckless and sorta free with his rope might get a heap worse reputation than what he deserves; and he gradually gets the blame for any stock disappearing within a couple of hundred miles from his stomping ground. Naturally that gets pretty deep under his hide, with the result that he figgers he might just as well live up to his reputation, 'cause if he gets caught "going south" with five hundred head he won't get hung any higher than he would for running off with just some old "ring boned" saddle horse.

Consequences is when the stock associations and others start to keep him on the move, he's using his *long rope* for fair, and when he's moving there's a few carloads of prime stock making tracks ahead of him. In Wyoming a few of the feud men tried to even scores that way; the hill billy was on horseback and toting a hair-trigger carbine.

I don't want to give the impression that the cattlemen started in the cow business by rustling, not by a long shot — they're plum against it in all ways, and most of 'em would let their herd dwindle down to none rather than brand anything lessen they're shure it's their own. But there is some what naturally hates to see anything go unbranded wether it's theirs or not, and being the critter don't look just right to 'em without said iron, they're most apt to plant one on and sometimes the brand don't always fit.

Like for instance, there was Bob Ryan riding mean horses all day and a lot of the night in all kinds of weather for somebody else at thirty a month and bacon. It wasn't any too interesting to him; he kinda hankered for a little range and a few head of stock of his own, and come to figgering that some outfits he'd rode for had no objections to their riders picking up a "slick" whenever it was safe. There was no reason much why them slicks couldn't just as well bear his own "iron," and that certain "ranny," being overambitious that way and sorta carefree, buys a few head of cows, calves, and yearlings, wherever he can get 'em and takes a "squatter" in the foothills, his weaning corrals being well hid higher up in some heavy timbered

The hill billy was on horseback and toting a hair-trigger carbine.

box canyon, and proceeds to drag a loop that makes him ashamed, at first.

There's the start of your cattle rustler — it's up to how wise he is, or how lucky, wether he keeps it up till he's really one or not. If he can get by till his herd is the size he wants it without getting caught, most likely he'll stop there and no one will know the difference, but if some inquisitive rider gets wind of his doings, and that wind scatters till it begins to look like a tornado, why it's liable to leave him in bad humor and make him somewhat more reckless.

A few months after Bob started on his own, a couple of riders out on circle was bringing in a bunch to the "cutting grounds," and in the "drags" noticed four cows with big bags bellering their heads off — and no calves. In another drive there's two more. Next morning, the range boss takes two riders with him, leaving the straw boss to take the others out on first "circle" — the six cows with the full bags was turned loose the night before and the boss finds 'em by a little corral in the brush still bellering (a cow and calf, if separated and losing track of one another, always return to where they'd last been together and wait for days till the one missing returns). There'd been a lot of cattle there and 'most impossible to track any special critter, so he goes up on a ridge toward the high mountains and "cuts" for tracks. A few miles to the north he runs across what he's looking for, and by the signs to be seen they sure must of been travelling and a horse track was there on top of the rest, looked a few days old.

Up a canyon it leads a ten or twelve miles, and they pass by Bob's camp, not seeing it. It was well hid and what's more, tracks is what the boss and the two riders was keeping their eyes on most — up a little further there's a corral and if it wasn't for them tracks it'd never be found. There'd been cattle there the night before, it was plain to see. They kept quiet and listened, off into the timber higher up a calf was heard and single file they climbed toward where it sounded to be from, when figgering they was close enough, they scattered and went three ways and on past around where the cattle was feeding till they got up above 'em, then joined one another; and getting off their horses they climbed a high point, squatted, took their hats off, and looking thru the cracks of a red rock, they could see a few of the cattle below 'em. Bob had 'em on feed and under cover during the day and in the corral at night till the brands healed. Nothing of *him* could be seen anywheres, but he was there keeping his eye on what he could see of the back-trail and at the same time standing "day herd" on the cattle.

Bob knew 'most any one would ride right up into the cattle, if in case they was looking for him figgerin' he'd be there, but he would of fooled 'em by just dropping off his perch into the other canyon and making distance — by the time they'd got thru looking for him he'd been in the next county. The boss reckoned on all that, being quite a hand on them sorta tricks himself at one time; so calculates the best thing to do is keep out of sight, circle around back to the corral, hide and wait till Bob brought

The end of a wrong start.

the cattle down and put up the poles at the gate. Along about sundown, the cattle is coming and Bob is with 'em, drives 'em into the corral, and he's putting up the last pole when from three different places at close distance he hears the command "Put up your hands," "'Way up there!" Bob reaches for the sky, knowing better than try to do different.

The next morning to the boss's surprise, there's no weaners in that corral; all grown stock mostly cows, and calves too young to be branded, but them cows had fresh irons and earmarks on 'em just beginning to heal. What was the original iron on them critters nobody could make out, it was blotched so bad and the ears cut so short that there was nothing to be seen but the *new iron*, that being sure visible and stretching from shoulder to hip-bone.

It was plain to see what Bob had been doing, but he had cattle of his own bearing the same iron, and he could prove it was of the first branding, and them weaners disappearing was a puzzle. The boss had a strong hunch he had 'em hid somewheres, but where? And how could he prove Bob did it?

Bob not being caught red-handed just lands into court and with his lawyer wins the fight; the judge and jury pronounces him "Not Guilty," and the lawyer takes the cattle for the fee. (It's 'most impossible to convict any one of cattle rustling, and that's why "necktie-parties" was so popular.) When the sun shines on his freedom again, the first thing that stares him in the eye is cattle once more, cattle everywhere on the hillsides and brakes — he knows

The stage-driver takes him and his "thirty
years' gathering" to the railroad station.

it's his move, so calculates to make the most of it while
moving. His idea is to clear enough to get him started in
some new country, where he ain't branded so well.

He knows he'll get the blame for all that disappears
in that territory, so he goes to work and takes pains to let
everybody know in the town and country that he's hitting
the breeze. He wants to let 'em understand that there'll
be a whole State, maybe two, between him and those
what suspicions. He sticks around for a week or more,
straightening out his affairs, and the while telling the folks
about him what a paradise this new country is where he's
going to, that he wouldn't come back again on a bet.

The stage-driver takes him and his "thirty years'
gathering" to the railroad-station and comes back telling

the storekeeper and livery-stable man that he's went for sure. He'd seen him buy a ticket for some town a thousand miles away, and everybody kinda draws a long breath saying something like "good riddance of bad rubbish."

Sure enough, Bob had went alright, and arrives at this new country unknown and walking kinda straight. The sheriff ain't ever heard of him and he inquires 'round at the stable where the headquarters for the Blue River Land and Cattle Company might be found. The superintendent, upon his asking for a job, informs him that he's full-handed excepting that he could use a good man "snapping broncs."

A few days later you could see Bob inside the breaking corral of the home ranch; four broncs are tied up and getting "eddicated" and another's saddled ready to be "topped off." He's standing there rolling a smoke, his mind not at all on the hobbled glass-eyed horse standing alongside him with legs wide apart and tipping the saddle near straight up with the hump that makes the boys ride. His eyes are on over and past the other broncs tied to the corral, and sees only away across the valley some fifteen miles. Timber out there draws his attention, and Bob wonders what the range is like at the perticular spot.

It's quite a ride for a green bronc, but not many days later you could see him winding up, following the cow trails to that timber and waterhole. He passes two "alkali licks" and rides on thru the aspens to the mesa — white sage, grama, and mountain bunch-grass everywhere, shadscale on the flat and wild peas in the gullies higher up.

He's rolling a smoke, his mind not at all on the hobbled glass-eyed horse standing alongside him.

There's a line of troughs at the waterhole and a few head of the Blue River cattle are watering there.

That night at the bunk house with the boys, Bob hazes the talk to drifting on about the springs and holdings of the company and by just listening, asking no questions, he finds that the little range he'd rode into that day was held by the outfit. He had a hunch they was holding it with no rights, and every one in the country had took it for granted it was theirs, never bothering about finding out.

A few months later the broncs are all "snapped out," a paycheck in Bob's chap pocket, and then pretty soon a log house is up and the smoke coming out of the fireplace thru the timber where the line of troughs and alkali licks was located. There was a howl from the company about somebody "jumping" one of their springs, but that don't do no good; saying they owned that range and proving it was two different things; and Bob stayed on, taking in horses to break at ten dollars a head and making a big bluff as to how much he's putting away, every so often.

One day Bob disappears and is gone for 'most six weeks; his place being out of the way of any riders nobody knows he'd went or returned, and if you'd asked him where he was keeping himself he'd said, "home." Anyway, in a few days after his return, he buys a hundred head of mixed stock, and some kinda wondered where he'd got the money to buy stock with, figgering even if he did make a good stake at breaking horses, it wouldn't buy one-fourth the cattle he'd paid cash for. He disappears once more without any one knowing of it and buys another little bunch of "dogies." Bob was getting bolder every time and the big outfits a thousand miles to the north and east was putting out a big reward for a cattle thief they didn't have the description of. They'd plumb forgot about Bob, knowing him to be south somewhere and doing well, as they'd hear tell from the riders travelling thru.

He got so he could change a brand on a critter, and with a broken blade and a little acid of his own preparation make that brand to suit his taste, and in fifteen minutes appear like it'd been there since the critter was born. You could feel the scaly ridge in the hide where the iron was supposed to've been and even a little white hair here and there; it would sure stand inspection from either the eye or the hand.

Bob knowing every hill, coulée, flat, creek, and river of that country, was a great help to him. He'd rode every foot of it for a hundred miles around. It was where he'd stood trial and lost his first herd. He knew the folks there had forgot him and that's what he wanted. It left him a clear trail out of suspicion; the train would take and leave him at some neighboring town at night getting a couple of ponies and hitting out on "jerky," a little flour, and salt before sun-up, he'd skirt the foothills and never would a rider get sight of him. Laying low by day and riding by night he'd locate the herds with the best beef and camp within a few miles of 'em so if they drifted he'd know their whereabouts and, soon as the weather permit, fog on behind 'em.

At the first sign of a strong wind, when tracks a few hours old are sifted over with fine sand, or before a first snow, you could see Bob getting his "piggin' string," unlimbering his ropes and testing his acid; his copper "running iron" was always with him too, hid between his saddle skirting and the lining; his 30-30 well cleaned and oiled and the old smoke wagon under his shirt and resting on his chap belt, he'd hit out on the best horse the country had for the herd he'd been watching, and go to cutting out a couple of carloads of the primest stuff he could get. Of course, by the time he'd get 'em to the shipping point, or market, they'd only be "feeders," but that brought a fair price.

The first night he'd camp on the critters' tails till they'd use all the energy they had to get out of the way. (In some cases it's been known of some cattle rustlers covering over forty miles single-handed with fifty some odd head in one night.) Bob had figgered a long time ahead the best way to take his cattle out, the hiding places for the day, and water to go with it, keeping shy of fences and ranches. At first sign of the rising sun his cattle was watered and taken up in some timbered canyon, the brands was worked over and a few hours later the herd was bedded down or feeding. The next night would be easier on both man and stock, and by the third, Bob felt pretty secure, but never would you

*He'd camp on the critters' tails till they'd used all
the energy they had to get out of the way.*

find him with the cattle during the day. The cattle being too tired to stray away was left soon as watered and taken on feed. When they'd be hid, Bob would "back-trail" a mile or so, where he could watch his cattle and see any riders what might be following him. In case there was, he had plenty of time before they got to his cattle and had 'em identified to make a getaway; for even tho' an "iron" may be worked over into another, the rustler ain't going to take a chance. There may be a "marker" in that bunch that only the owner, or the riders familiar with the cattle, would recognize; and that's enough to entitle the rustler to the stout limb and a piece of rope if he's caught.

When once out of the stolen cattle's territory and a hundred miles or so farther the cattle are loaded into the cars. (It's done at night if there is no inspection in that particular State.) Bob's going to stick to the finish 'cause he figgers his iron is going to stand the inspection of the stockyards inspector — he can show you where that brand is recorded and that they're his cattle unless you have reason to be real out of the ordinary inquisitive and want to know too much — but even then Bob has cattle bearing the same "iron" on his range to the south, and it may be mighty hard to prove they're not his. Furthermore, nobody knows or can prove he's been out of the country or whether he's shipped some of his own cattle or not — and no one had seen him around where the cattle was stolen.

It was getting real interesting, and he did not realize that he was taking a liking to stealing cattle and making clean getaways. The herd at his home camp was getting to be just a bluff, bearing half a dozen different recorded irons and earmarks. He was beginning to use them to fall back on in case investigation was made and traced back to his "hangout." He'd made three trips to Chicago and was just thinking of settling down to steal no more. He knew this good luck wouldn't last, and besides, picking up a few "orejanas" now and again around his own little range to the south might prove just as interesting; but the fever had him, with the result that he found out no matter how close you figger there's always something you'll overlook what'll give you away.

He started north for another raid, and thought he'd take his own saddle horses along this time, being that good horses are hard to pick up everywhere that way. There was one horse especially he hated to leave behind. It was a big blood bay, bald-faced and stocking-legged, and when he got to his destination to the north, and the stock car was being switched at the yards, one of the old timers recognized the horse and kept mum till Bob came to the stock car and led him out with his other horse. Ten minutes later Bob was feeding up at the "open-all-night" Chink restaurant and watching the front door. The sheriff comes thru the kitchen and when Bob turned around to his "ham and eggs" there was the muzzle of a "45" staring him in the eye.

He lost his second herd to the same lawyer and faced the same judge of two years before. He'd only stole one horse where he'd got away with over two hundred head of cattle in that country, but that one horse put the kibosh on him. There was no proof that he'd stole any cattle, but they suspicioned mighty strong; and they couldn't of handed him any more if they could of proved it. So figgering on killing two birds with one stone, the judge, not weeping any, throws the book at him, which means he gives Bob the limit.

If Bob would of had better luck the first time he tried to settle down in the country where he'd made such a bad "reputation" for himself, most likely by now he'd been just a prosperous cowman and kept his "long ropes" to home. I don't figger Bob was bad, just a little too anxious to have something, and later on getting too much satisfaction in outwitting others. Any stranger was welcome to Bob's camp to feed and rest up; a fresh horse, or anything else he had, was offered to them what needed it, and it wouldn't matter if your pack horse was loaded with gold nuggets they was just as safe in his bunk house, or maybe safer, than in the safety vault. His specialty was cattle and he got to love to use his skill in changing irons.

He was just like a big average of the Western outlaw and cattle rustler; his squareness in some things made up for his crookedness in others. There was no petty work done: saddle, spurs, and chaps was safe hanging over the corral, but there was one thing you had to keep away from in the rustler's doings; if you saw at a distance a smoke going up, one man with a critter down and a horse standing rope's length away, it's always a good idea to ride 'way around and keep out of sight, unless you want your Stetson perforated. If you was interested and had company, why that's another story.

I used to know a big cowman, who'd been fairly free with the running iron at one time and had done a heap of rustling. Many a head he'd lost in the same way afterward. Those he caught was dealt mighty hard with, and he'd expected the same if he'd ever made that fatal mistake, but he was lucky enough not to.

One day a "nester," what had drifted in from the other side of the plains and settled on one of his creek bottoms, finds himself and family run out of bacon or any sort of meat. He ups and shoots a fine yearling, takes the hindquarters, and leaves the rest in the hide

A man with a critter down, his horse standing rope's length away, is a good thing to keep away from – unless you want to get your Stetson perforated.

for the coyotes, or to spoil. One of the riders runs onto the carcass, and lucky there was no proof of who done it, for that kind of doings sure gets a "rise" from a cowhand. A little over a month later, another yearling is butchered the same way, but the hide is gone and that's what makes it interesting.

It was found under the nester's little haystack. There's nobody home just then. The cowman finding this evidence had changed many an iron and earmark in his early start (as I've mentioned before) but never had he played hog and left any perfectly good beef to spoil on the range, and he figgers to teach that country spoiling hombre a few lessons in range etiquette. About sundown, he catches up with him and family just when the wagon and team reaches the musselshell bottoms where there's fine big cottonwoods. A carbine stares the nester in the face, and at the same time the cowman produces a piece of the hide bearing his iron and asks him to account for it. The man on the wagon is too scared to speak or move, so is the rest back of the seat.

The cowman uncoils his rope, plays with it a while, and pretty soon a little "wild cat" loop settles neat and around that waster's neck, he's drug off his seat and close to one of them natural gallows, the rope is throwed over a limb, picked up again on the other side, and taking his "dallies" to the saddle horn, the cowman goes on till that farmer's big feet are just about a yard off the ground, a squawk is heard from the wagon and the whole family runs up to plead for the guilty party.

A little "wild cat" loop settles neat and around that waster's neck, he's jerked off his seat and drug to the nearest cottonwood.

They plead on for quite a spell but the cowman acts determined and hard of hearing. When it's gone far enough and that nester gets blue 'round the gills, the rope slacks up and he sprawls down to earth; the cowman is right atop of him and tells him he's got his family to thank for to see the sun come up again, "and if I ever catch you leaving meat of my stock to spoil on the range again I'll get you up so far you'll never come down, family or no family"; and he winds up with "*you can kill all of my beef you need*, but just what you need and no more, do you hear? And I want you to produce the hides of them beeves too, every one of 'em."

With that he rides off, and the nester's family is still trying to figger out what kind of folks are these "cow persons," anyway.

Chapter V

WINTER MONTHS
IN A COW CAMP

It took me a long time to figger out anywheres near of what I'd done with my summer's wages. I know I'd bought me a few winter clothes and paid out for a couple of weeks of livery stable board for my horse; then the hotel bill besides some real fancy meals had took a lot of my money. I'd bought the rounds when my turn came and stepped out with the boys, and even though I was breathing sober steady ever since I hit town, I couldn't for the life of me make out how that money went so fast. I'd saved it careful too that summer before, even rode my old saddle and made it do till the shipping was done so I could manage to live a life of ease for the few winter months.

Riding them winter months didn't strike me as anything cheerful no more, and I thought that this once I'd be able to hole in comfortable for that snowy cold period; but my pockets sprung a leak, and being that I

Stone Pile Camp.

couldn't get no comfort of what was past and spent, I begins to look into the future and wonders what cow outfit would hire a cowboy this time of year. I'm running the irons of the outfits I know of through my mind and looking into the future real deep, when I raises up straight in my bed and looks out of the hotel window to see snow coming down and adding up on the fourteen inches already on the level. Yep! I figgers the range will be needing riders.

I finds myself whistling some as I clean up, and somehow and another when I comes down the steps into the hotel lobby it don't look like much to me. There's a few tinhorn gamblers with the "hop head" complexion sticking around, and a couple of fat slick-looking gents a-swapping jokes by the big stove. I steps up to the bar, gets me a eye opener on my looks and sashays out in the dining room, where I figgers on throwing a bait to hold me till I reaches my next stopping place.

My ham and eggs is down to half when old Tom Meyers, superintendent of the "hip-O," steps up and asks how I'm setting. "Pretty fair," I says and don't tell him none of my plans, thinking that he's full handed anyway. I don't show where I'm at all interested when he says he's needing of a man at "Stone Pile" camp. "It's mean weather out right now," I says, "and I'm afraid I'm getting kinda soft, but how much are you paying?"

With a month's wages handed to me in advance
I pays my bills at the hotel, bar, and stable (they
hadn't been running long) and it feels kinda good
to be riding out again even if the snow was deep
and more of it was coming. My horse was a sniffing
of it and lining out full of life. After the long spell
in the stall he was glad to be out and going
somewhere, and somehow I wasn't a bit sorry either.

A couple of days and along what I figgered to
be about sundown (it was still snowing and the wind
was coming up) I reaches the camp where I'm to get
my winter horses and ride from. There's three or
four rolls of bedding belonging to boys what'd *stayed
to town* for the winter (same as I'd figgered on doing)
and I uses one of 'em till I can get my own roll.

There's two ranch hands at the camp shovelling
hay to near a thousand head of "hospital cattle"
(weak stock), besides a cook and a rider not counting
me, and the next morning when I sniffs and smells
the bacon from my bunk I know that I've settled
down to some tall hard work.

It's still dark when I saddles my horse and lines
out. I'd rode that country many times before and
knowed how and where the cattle was running. The
dry stock was in good condition, outside the few
old stuff and cows with calves and "leppies" (orphant
calves) what are to be brought in and fed.

Along about noon I have a few bunches spotted
what had weak ones in and starts back for camp,

cutting 'em out as I go and driving 'em along making about a mile an hour. Them being weak and the snow being deep it ain't long till they begin to get tired, and me knowing that the less I rush 'em the better time I'll make, I'm driving 'em easy and keeps 'em just barely moving. As the driving is kept up and the cattle want to rest they begin to spread like a fan, heading all directions, and I have a hard time keeping 'em together; but taking it real easy manages to get 'em a half a mile closer to camp, when a couple of dogies on the outside begin to get on the "prod" (fight), which means it's time for me to quit.

I had twelve head in that bunch and it took me six hours to drive 'em about five miles. It was way after dark when I dropped 'em and hit for camp, and I still had a good ten miles to go.

It takes me three days to bring 'em in, and the end of the third and late again finds me pushing a mighty weak, tired bunch of dogies through the gates of the feed yard at the camp and headed for the big shelter sheds. Half of 'em was wanting to fight but when they see the hay what was spread and waiting for 'em they kind of forgot I was around and went to eating.

For a spell that kind of work kept on. There was days when we'd be drifting with the herds and the blizzard a-howling full force, when you could hardly see your hand in front of you and the only way you knowed the direction you was headed was by the wind. If that wind switched to another direction without you knowing of it (you wasn't apt to know in the blinding storm) you was running good chances of getting lost unless you run acrost some landmark what told of your whereabouts.

The snow drifted and piled high but in drifting it cleared some ridges, and there's where the strong cattle along with the range horses was finding their feed.

Then the weather cleared and stayed a steady cold. Me and the other cowboy had covered the whole country and hazed in all what needed feed; riding was getting easy.

And one day when we hear of a dance what was going to be pulled off at the crossing we figger there could be no better time for it to happen; so saddling up our private ponies us two boys and the cook set out for the crossing forty miles away. Too bad the ranch hands couldn't come, being they had to shovel so much hay *every day*, no more and no less, but they was good enough to let the cook go, remarking that if they couldn't get away they wouldn't keep anybody else from it.

We covered that forty miles and got to the other end in plenty time for the big midnight feed. We had our ears all wrapped up to keep 'em from freezing off, but, along with the coyotes howling to the moon, we could hear old Darb a-see-sawing on his fiddle and somebody else calling the dance a half a mile before we reached the house.

Lights was in every room and the smoke was coming straight up through three different chimneys; so we spurred up our ponies and rode towards the stack yards where we turned 'em loose.

We just enters the house as we hear a "tag" dance announced and by the time our chaps, spurs, and extra clothes are took off it's half over, but not too late to tag a couple of hombres, take their ladies, and dance some till *we* got tagged ourselves. When the dance was through the blood was beginning to circulate some, and by the time we shook hands all around we was more than ready to help keep things cheerful.

Half the crowd was cow-punchers from everywhere, a few cowmen with their families, from the oldest down to the weaner (what was left in the bedroom but made itself heard now and again), then a few boys from town what sleighed over and brought a few girls along. There was about six men to each lady, and it was always a wonder to me how the supposed to be weaker sex could tire the men even at that, but they did, and the fatter they was the longer they stayed.

The big feed at midnight and specially that coffee was a life saver to most of us what come in late; and when the fiddler resumed his playing there was no quitting till daybreak. The ladies all disappeared then, and us boys would take the floor and go on with the stag dance; if "fire-water" was around that stag dance was apt to be kind of rough and end up in wrestling matches.

Games and tricks of all kinds are tried: none are easy but some are done, and when that lags down there may be two young fellers in the corner what'd been visiting the bottom of the manger too often and arguing or betting on riding; more bets are put in from the outside crowd just to make things interesting.

The bunch all heads for the corrals and a wall-eyed rangy bronc is led out, saddled, straddled, and with the bawling of that bronc bucking away with a whooping rider fanning him, the crowd hollering "stay with him, cowboy" or the like, the sun is coming up, the ladies are waking, and the end of the doings have come.

Breakfast is spread and all hands, after partaking of the bait, are talking of hitting the trail. Ponies are caught, harnessed or saddled, and with a lot of howdedo the crowd is leaving for their home grounds.

My bronc was "high-lifed" as I go through the corral gate and bucks right through the calf pen, same as it wasn't there, near hooking on the corner of the stable as he goes by; but a mile further on he cools down some and the boys catch up with me.

We're riding along a ways, when Dan remarks, "I feel something in the air." A light breeze had sprung up from the west, and come to think about it, it felt a whole lot as if a chinook was headed our way, and as we ride on that breeze keeps a-getting warmer and stronger. The deep snow was already beginning to show the effects and sagging as the warm wind et its way through.

My bronc was "high-lifed" – goes to bucking and near
hooks me on the corner of the stable as he goes by.

The next day as I ride out of camp the chinook is blowing for sure, and when I strikes the first bunch of cattle I found them to be as I was afraid I would. They'd been strong and rustling fine a few days before; they'd been on their feet steady through the cold weather, not hankering to lay down in the snow, and the exercise kept the blood circulating; but the chinook had took the snow off a few spots on the ridges and at them spots is where I finds most of the stock laying down and all the life out of 'em.

They was hardened to the cold and the sudden warmth left 'em so weak that only half of 'em can get up as I rides in on 'em. I spends a couple of hours helping the weakest ones by "tailing 'em up," and steadying 'em some afterwards so they can navigate. I'm working hard 'cause I know that when the chinook quits blowing and it gets cold again them cattle what are down now will get stiff and cramped, the blood'll quit circulating, and the critter's legs will be plumb useless, which leaves 'em good only for coyote bait.

"Tailing up" is an awful hard and ungrateful job too, the critter treats you the same as if you was a bear or a wolf what's come to eat her alive, and proceeds to try and hook you, and, wild-eyed, bellers in your ear how she'd like to tear you up. You help her along and she struggles to get on her feet, not so that she might be able to rustle and live but just to get a chance to run you down. Sometimes she works hard enough that she forgets what she was going to do when she did get on footing again,

"Tailing up" is mighty hard, and the critter is never grateful.

and if you can sneak away using her body to keep her from seeing you and get on your horse before she sees, everything may be O. K.; but, if she happens to turn her head and glance back as you're making your getaway, she might remember what she wanted to do to you a while ago *and try it.* She'll let out a bellering war whoop and forget that she's kinda shaky in the knees, and is apt to turn and try to get to you too quick, which makes her do a spraddling nose dive. Down again, and there to stay unless you help her up once more and make a success of your getting away.

I've tailed up one critter as often as half a dozen times before I could leave without her taking after me and falling down again. Then I'd have to hang my coat (when I had one with me) over her horns and blindfold her that way till I'd get to my horse. Once in the saddle I'd ride by her, get the coat back and be away before she'd know what happened.

Well, I kept a-riding the bare ridges that day and getting cattle on their feet and moving. The next day was the same and the chinook was still a-blowing and eating up the snow. Half of it is already melted away and water is running down the coulées to the creeks, making 'em the size of rivers. Any stranger would of thought sure that spring'd come sudden, but I knowed the cowmen was losing sleep for worrying, more afraid of the harm the hard freeze would do to the stock after the chinook'd left than the chinook itself could do while it was blowing.

Along about the middle of the afternoon I meets with the other rider; I sees he's near all in as he pulls up his horse and goes to rolling a smoke, but he's smiling some as he remarks that these winter jobs sure do get aggravating at times. We had pretty well all of our cattle up and a-going again and it was about time, 'cause we could feel the air getting cooler and the breeze was shifting to the north. The snow'd quit melting and the creeks was getting down to creek size again. "I'm thinking to-night is going to put a crimp in some of the stock," Dan says as we start out for some draws to the west where we figgered to find the few bunches of cattle we'd missed in our circles.

It's good and dark by the time we head our horses towards camp and it was getting colder every minute.

The wet snow was freezing through solid and in lots of places the top crust would hold our horses. "I wouldn't be surprised," I says, "but what the Old Man (meaning the superintendent) might have to either ship the stock south to pull 'em through the winter, that is if they can make it to the railroad, or else ship some feed in and haul it out here to 'em; that would be some expensive too. The bad shape the range is in now with all the good feed buried in solid ice, something'll sure have to be done or else the outfit'll find itself with more cowboys than cattle when spring does come."

"Sure," Dan says, "and for my part I wouldn't mind hitting south with the stock 'cause I feel like I could stand some warmer climate myself." And rubbing his ears he puts his horse into a lope remarking that we'd better be drifting if we want anything to eat that's warm.

The Cypress Cattle Company was running over thirty thousand head of cattle; three thousand of 'em was at Stone Pile camp, where Dan and me was riding, the rest was at other cow camps, and a big herd at the home ranch, where there was other riders and hay shovellers looking after 'em. At our camp there was enough hay put up the summer before to feed and pull through the winter about fifteen hundred head of stock. The other fifteen hundred was supposed to rustle. They could easy enough and come out strong in the spring after any average winter, 'cause the stock what was left out on the range to rustle through was all dry stuff and steers. Cows with calves and weaners and all old or weak stock was fed from the start of the bad weather till spring breakup.

The weather kept clear and cold; the little glass tube outside our camp by the door was saying from thirty to thirty-five below, and had been keeping that up for about a week. Lucky, we thought, the wind wasn't blowing then or every critter would of froze stiff where they stood. We kept on bringing in the weakest and only them what really needed feed the most. There was many more should been brought in but the last week made us fill the feed yards, so that it wouldn't be wise to bring them in. There was enough hay to feed fifteen hundred head till spring and it was better, we thought, to keep on feeding just them and take a chance on letting the stronger pull through on the outside, than feed two thousand or more and run out of hay at the wrong time and lose 'em all.

It didn't look like there was going to be any shipping done either way. No super or cow boss showed up to see how the stock was coming and we figgered that old timers like they was, and never forgetting the days when there wasn't a hoof fed, they'd decided to take a chance like they'd done many a winter before and hope that the weather would change in some way in time to save the stock. And as luck would have it the weather did change.

It was near three weeks since the chinook'd come and left the range a field of ice and crusted snow with the few bare spots that helped some keeping the cattle alive. The willows on the creek bottoms and the sage was all et down to the ice, and, outside of the few branches what was too big for them to tackle, the country was clean as a whistle. There was little bunches of range horses here and there and even though they was having a hard time of it, it was some easier for them 'cause they could paw out their feed where the critter could only root with her nose. But along the trails the horses would make where they pawed up the hard snow and broke the crust with their hoofs, you could see the cattle following and picking what the horses would leave.

Big hunks of crusted snow had been pawed out and turned up for the feed underneath, but as they was loosened the grass came out with the hunks and left only bare ground.

The stock had so little feed in 'em that it looked like their flanks was near touching the backbone, but the most of 'em was strong and if it hadn't been for that chinook they would now be in good shape.

Anyway the weather changed and for the best. We didn't think it for the best at first 'cause the change was for *another chinook* and they as a rule don't leave nothing but bone piles unless they come late in the spring, and this was only February. For forty-eight hours it blowed warm. Dan and me was doing our bestest riding, and tailing up for all we was worth every critter what had to be helped on her feet. We'd remark that it'd be for the last time 'cause we was sure afraid of what the cold that 'most always follows a chinook would do to 'em.

It started clouding up before the chinook quit, and that's when our hopes come back. The snow was 'most all gone to water and running down the draws; the country was left bare and brown and the cattle weaker than ever, but feed a-plenty was in sight and easy to get at, and clouding up as it was with the wind dying down gives us to understand that there won't be no real cold weather coming right soon anyway.

It stayed warm and in a couple of days it started to snow, kinda wet at first, but she stuck and kept on a-coming, slow but sure and steady. The cloudy weather was with us for a good two weeks and gradually getting colder, when it cleared again and the thermometer went down to ten below. There was near a foot of snow on the ground again and the cattle was having a hard time rooting down to the feed, but the slow drop of the thermometer and the chance at some feed before the snow came recuperated 'em some. A few more had to be brought in and we did it, taking big chances of running out of hay too soon.

And then another six inches of snow piled up on top of the foot already down, which makes us and the hay shovellers do a heap of figgering as to how we was going to pull the stock through. The hay was fed and handled real careful but it was dwindling away fast; two thousand of the hungry critters was in the feed pens eating up the hay what was supposed to carry not over fifteen hundred head.

And by all appearances it looked like the "hospital stuff" would have to be fed another six weeks before we could call 'em pulled through. Dan and me was doing our darnedest not to bring in any more than we could help and coaxing 'em along to stand up and rustle where they was, but there was times right along every day when we'd have to come in with a few more.

Spring was late, it still looked like the middle of winter, and we had to contend not only with the usual few winter calves but spring calves was beginning to pop up here and there and showing their little white faces. The daggone coyotes was the only animal getting fat, and it sure used to do my heart a lot of good to keel one of 'em over just when he'd be doing some tall sneak on some poor little feller of a calf when his mammy was too far away or too weak to get there in time to do any protecting.

Like one day riding along and keeping tab on the weak ones as usual, I runs across a cow-track in the snow. A little baby calf was trying mighty hard to keep up with her and a little further on there's two other kinds of tracks joins in and follows. They're big tracks, too big for coyotes, and I concludes they must be gray wolves. Now I know that as a rule wolves wouldn't tackle them only maybe just for the want to kill, or when horses is getting scarce.

Anyway, I know *I* sure like to get 'em *any time I can* no matter what they're after, and spurs up on the trail, the 30-30 carbine right in my hands and the business end of it pointed straight ahead. Daggone 'em, they *are* after that cow and calf. I can see that plain enough by the signs in the snow where she'd stopped, made a stand and went on for some place (I figgered) where she could back up alongside a cliff or something and have only one side to watch from.

I can see the wolves are only after a little excitement 'cause they could of killed both her and the calf right there and then if they'd wanted to. Instead, they just let her go and kept on aggravating her as she went. I thought to myself if they're so rearing for excitement, I'd sure be glad to oblige 'em that way when I catches up.

The trail heads on for the foot-hills; I'm keeping my horse into a high lope, and slacks up only when topping ridges, so I won't bump into the little party and queer things before I can get into action. I want to see them before they see me.

I finally spots 'em a half a mile to the right. There's a ridge between us, and soon as I get a peek of their whereabouts and the lay of the land, what little I showed of myself is out of sight again. I seen where the mother'd found a good spot to make her *last stand*, and, even tho' she knowed how the fight was going to end, she was sure making use of the rim-rock she'd backed up against, and bellering for help that didn't seem to come.

I can see by the signs in the snow where she'd stopped and made a stand.

Hell bent for election I follows up the draw I'm in to where I figger I'd better hoof it the rest of the way. There was no wind to give me away, and I manages to crawl up to within fifty yards of the fighting bunch, taking in at a glance all what'd been going on while I'm looking down the rifle sights.

The wolves are enjoying themselves so much that they're not on the look-out as they generally are. They had the cow down and letting her last as long as they could without allowing the fight to get too monotonous. Her head and horns are still a-going and mighty dangerous to anything what comes near. The poor little calf was all together as yet, and off a ways, plumb helpless and watching, too young to know for sure what to do. The wolves had figgered him not worth while to fool with right then. They'd fix his mammy first, spend a few minutes with him afterwards, and then go on to the next victim.

And right there I stopped one of 'em with a bullet right through him from shoulder to shoulder. The other started to run and I lets him have a pill too, but he kept on a-running, dragging two useless hind legs; his back was broke. A couple more shots what don't seem to affect him none and I gets my horse, takes after him, and brings him back, limp, with a bullet between his ears.

I gathers up little Johnny (calf), puts his dying mammy out of misery, and being I'm not very far from camp, I don't stop to skin the wolves right then but takes 'em in as they are. Tying their hind legs together I throws 'em over the back of the saddle, gets on myself and pulls the little "leppy" up in front of me. My horse don't quite agree to all the load and specially objects to wolves, but I finally talks him into being good enough to take us the little ways to camp.

Two more weeks gone, and it still looks and feels like the middle of winter, when by rights of season the range ought to be getting bare of snow and the grass showing a

My horse don't quite agree to all the load and specially objects to wolves.

little green; and worse yet, the hay is all gone and fed up, every speck of it.

There was a little horse hay, but that little bit wouldn't mean nothing to all them hungry cattle, and besides them horses had to work and help save them same cattle, and they had to be well fed to do that work.

So it seems to us that the outfit is up against it for sure. We know that no hay can be bought nowheres around, being they've all got their own stock to save and running short themselves. Dan and me had just about give up thinking of some way out, when of a sudden it comes to me, and I remembers of how one time up in Alberta a cowman saved his stock and pulled 'em through in good shape with a six-horse team and a drag (or snow-plough).

No more thought of than tried. There was enough harness in the stables to hook up thirty head of horses, and two teams on hand and ready; but we wanted two six-horse teams to do the work and we was short eight head; so Dan and me hits out looking through every bunch of horses on the range for anything what had collar marks, and any of 'em what had was run in and put to work. It didn't matter whether they belonged to the outfit or not.

Two V-shaped drags was made out of heavy logs with thick planks nailed on the outside so it'd push the snow away on both sides and clean. We get the teams all hooked up, straightened around, and we're ready to go. It worked fine, and the grass wherever we went and drug was easy to get. The snow hadn't drifted any and was no thicker in the draws than on the ridges, so we worked the draws and found plenty of the good strong feed our cattle was needing so bad.

We had to cover a lot of country and keep a-going so that they'd all get some; but the exercise and rustling, along with that feed they was getting, made 'em some stronger, and it wasn't but a few days when the cattle all knowed what them V-shaped logs dragging along meant.

The strongest ones would follow 'em right up for a ways, and we'd come down the same draw but on the other side. The leaders would stop and feed, leaving the weaker cattle have a chance as we come by.

That'd been going on for about two weeks; the stock wasn't picking up no fat but they was making out all right. The ranch-hands handled the drags and Dan and me was riding, still bringing a few weak ones from the outside stuff every once in a while.

May was getting near now and sure enough spring ought to show itself pretty quick if it's going to show up at all; but as Dan remarked to me and says, "Bill, this damn country ain't got no spring or summer to speak of; it's eight months winter and four months cold weather," and I begins to think he was right.

But the days was getting longer and the sun stronger, and pretty soon it begins to get warmer, and after a while I notices at the edge of where the snow'd been scraped of that the grass was getting green. It looked so good that I come near eating some.

It wasn't but a few days when the cattle all knowed what them V-shaped logs dragging along meant.

Then one morning as I'm saddling up, a light breeze hits me, and it's coming from the southwest. After that it didn't take long; it started to melt and get warm but not so warm that it'd weaken the cattle too much. The snow-plough was put away and instead of bringing in weak stock any more we'd spend our time tailing up what few felt the effects of the coming warm weather.

We was beginning to see little white and brockle-faced calves sunning themselves everywhere and their mammies right close was filling up on the half green buffalo grass, picking up steady on fat and strength.

The gray wolves was hitting out for the tall timber and the coyotes had to be satisfied with gophers once more.

Spring had come.

Chapter VI

The Makings of
a Cow-horse

A month or so before the round-up wagons pull out, the raw bronc (unbroke range horse) is enjoying a free life with the "stock horses" (brood-mares and colts). He's coming four years old marked by the first signs of spring. A few warm days starts him shedding, and just as the green grass is beginning to peek out from under the snow and living is getting easier, why here comes a long lanky rider on a strong grain-fed horse and hazes him and the bunch he's with into the big corrals at the home-ranch.

He's cut out with a few more of his age and put into a small round corral — a snubbing post is in the centre — and showed where, according to the rope marks around it, many such a bronc as him realized what they was on this earth for.

The big corral gate squeaks open and in walks the long lanky cowboy packing two ropes; one of them ropes sneaks up and snares him by the front feet just when he's making a grand rush to get away from it. He's flattened to the ground and that other rope does the work tying him down. A hackamore is slipped on his head while the bronc is still wondering what's happened, and from the time he's let up for a sniff at the saddle he's being eddicated, so that when the wagon pulls out a few weeks later his first promotion comes, and he's classed as "saddle-stock."

From then it's 'most all up to what kind of a head that pony's got whether he'll get on further than being just a saddle-horse. He may have to be pulled around a lot to get anything out of him towards what he should do, or on the other hand, he may take to it easy and get down to learning of his own accord after his bucking spells are over with.

He'll get all the time he needs to catch onto the new ropes of cow work, and only one thing at a time will be teached to him so that he'll not be rattled, but first, his bucking is what the rider'll object to and try to break him out of, and every time he bogs his head for that perticular kind of orneriness that bronc is apt to get his belly-full of the quirt.

But the cow-foreman has no place on the outfit he's running for any such hombre what don't treat the ponies right, and if a cowboy is kept on the pay-roll what naturally is rough on horse-flesh he'll get a string of horses cut to

One of them ropes sneaks up and snares him by the front feet just when he's making a grand rush to get away from it.

him that's just as mean as he is and fight him right back, or even go him one better whenever the chance shows up.

There's horses though that has to be rough handled, born fighters what'll do just the opposite of what they should do to be good; they want to be ornery and them kind calls only for the real rough bronco fighter what'll fight 'em to a finish.

Them's the kind of horses what makes up a "rough-string"; every cow outfit has 'em. Them horses'll range in age from five-year-old colts what craves fighting on up to fifteen and twenty-year-old outlaws; they 'most always keep one man in the hospital steady, and when he comes out the other man is about due to take his place either with the nurses or the angels.

The good, patient "bronc twister" what takes pains to teach the bronc to be good and be a real cow-horse don't as a rule have anything to do with the "rough-string"; his patience and ability with horses is too valuable to the company to have it go to waste on outlaws. So his work comes in on the uneddicated colt (the raw bronc), trying in all ways to hold the good what's in him, at the same time keeping his spirit intact, and talk him out of being ornery, if he can.

Like for instance, that long lanky cowboy and the raw bronc I mentioned in the first part of this writing; they both have a mighty good chance of getting along fine with one another. If they do, that same bronc'll be rode out on circle and learn the ways of the critter, when later on he'll be turned over to another hand. The older cowboy, what's past hankering for "rough edges" on them broncs, will then take him and proceed to ride and help him along with his learning.

Then's when the good or the bad in him will come out to stay; at that time he knows the human enough to tell what to expect, and if he wants to be good he's got a mighty good chance, the same if he wants to be bad, for this older hand is not hankering to get in no mix-up; the pony feels that, and *if* he's bad at heart he'll sure take advantage of it and buffalo the older cowboy to turning him loose or else buck him off in the hills somewhere.

If he succeeds in running his bluff once he'll feel sure that he can do it with every man what tries to handle him, and if he can fight wicked enough it might be hard to show him different. Consequences is, if that confidence ain't taken out of him right sudden it'll take hold on him with the result that he lands in the "rough-string" and the promotion stops there, — one more what has to be tied down before he can be saddled.

But, being as I said before that this raw bronc and the long lanky cowboy had mighty good chances of getting along fine, I'll let the good win out the same as it did with this perticular little horse I been trying to write about ever since I started this.

This little horse weighed around eleven hundred pounds and all in one hunk; what I mean is each part of him knowed what the other part was going to do and followed up according, without a kink nowheres. In bucking, or running, he'd make you wonder if he was horse-flesh or dynamite. Just an ordinary horse to look at though, chunky, short back and short ankles, but with a deep chest, and that head promised a lot either way he went.

That day I run him in, throwed him, and slipped the hackamore on his head, a name for him came to me just as natural as though I'd been thinking of one for hours. "Brown Jug," and that sure fit him all the way through even to the color; also like the jug he had plenty of "kick" in him.

From the first saddling he didn't disappoint me none, for he went after me and sure made me ride; in order to stay I had to postpone fanning him for a spell and thought I was doing real well to be able to do that much. It was just my luck that none of the boys was around to see me put up such a ride on such a horse; I told 'em about it, but, to the way it struck me, that was mighty tame compared to how it really was, and the next day when some of them boys happened around just as I was climbing Brown Jug again, the little son of a gun just crowhopped around and acted like he loved me and my rigging 'most to death.

He bucked at every setting each day after that for about ten days; then one day as I was going through the corral gate to give him his daily "airing," he "went to pieces" right there at the gate, and where it was slick with ice he fell hard and flat on his side and smashed one of my stirrups.

Naturally the first thing came to my mind was to hold him down for a spell and see if I was caught anywheres in the rigging. I wasn't. Then I thinks that now would be a good time to teach *his kind* of a horse how bucking wasn't at all nice, so I proceeds to tie him down. That don't hurt a horse, only his feelings, specially so when interrupted that way in the middle of the performance.

I'd whipped him some while bucking a few days before and I found out before I was through that his kind had to be handled different, 'cause he bucked and showed fight all the way through and never let up till he was tired out, then he went to sulking. After that I watched my chance for some other way to break him out of it.

My chance came when he fell and I didn't let it slip by. I gave him a good half-hour to think it over, and when I let him up, me a-setting in the saddle, he was glad to get away from the forced rest and be able to stand on his pins again; but he was sure took down a peg, and when I loped him out sudden he seemed to've forgot that was the time he liked to buck best.

There was twelve broncs in my string, each was getting short rides on "inside circle," or at the cutting grounds. Their teaching came right along with the cattle and the average of them colts was coming fine, but Brown Jug was ahead of 'em all and naturally I helped him all the more.

I gave him a good half-hour to think it over.

He'd bucked only once since I tied him down and that second time he didn't get to buck like he wanted to then; he'd only made a half a dozen jumps, when I reached down on one rein, pulled his head up and jerked his feet out from under him, laying him down again just when he wanted to be in action the most.

That fixed him for good, and I figgered if he'd ever buck again it'd be when he got cold and wanted to warm up, or when somebody'd tickle him with the spur at the wrong time. Well, if he did it'd only show he had feelings and the kind of spirit that makes the cow-horse.

It was a couple of weeks since Brown Jug'd bucked last; it was out of his system by now and I was beginning to take a lot of interest in the ways of handling the critter. I kept him in my string long as I could; then one day the foreman, who'd been watching with an eagle eye the work of every colt I'd been breaking, figgered the "raw edge" was pretty well took off them broncs and fit to be divided up amongst the boys for easy work.

The next morning I'm ready to leave the wagon behind, also the ponies I'd broke, and hit back for the home-ranch on a gentle horse, where I'm to round up another string of raw broncs and start in breaking fresh. But before leaving I manages to get the foreman to one side. "Now Tom," I says, "there's one special little horse in them broncs I'm turning over what has the makings of a 'top-horse' and I'd sure like to see a real good man get him, a man that'll make him what he promises to be. I know Flint Andrews would sure like to have him, and I'm asking as a favor if you'd see that Flint gets Brown Jug."

"You surprise me, Bill," he says, squinting over Brown Jug's way, then back at me, "why I thought all horses was alike to you no matter how good or bad they be; but I guess I thought wrong, and if you'd like to see Flint get the brown horse don't worry about it, he'll get him."

"That's the trouble being a bronc peeler and working for them big cow outfits," I says to my horse as I'm riding along back to the ranch; "a feller don't no more than begin to get interested in the way the colts are learning; and just about the time the orneriness is took out of 'em and they're behaving fine they're took away and scattered along in the other boys' strings, and another bunch of green, raw, fighting broncs takes their place."

I'm at the ranch near three weeks and coming along pretty fair with the new bunch when the wagons begin pulling in. The spring round-up was over with, and three of the four "remudas" was being corralled one after another; cow-horses, night-horses, and circle-horses was being cut out and turned on the range to rest up till the next spring, over five hundred head of 'em, and the other two hundred was put in the pasture to keep going till fall round-up. Them was the colts what'd just been "started" that spring along with the "spoiled horses" what belonged most to the "rough-string," and needed steady setting on in order to make 'em good.

Brown Jug came in with one of the remudas and was looking fine. Flint couldn't get to me quick enough to tell me what a great little horse he was, and how near he could come to being human. "Never kettled (bucked) once," he says, "and I never saw a horse getting so much fun out of beating a critter at her own game as he does; he sure camps on their hocks from start to finish."

A few days later I had a chance to watch him at work. Flint was a-talking away to him and that little son of a gun of a horse seemed to understand everything he said and talk right back with them ears and eyes of his. I was getting jealous of what Flint could do with

Brown Jug, and it set me down a peg to see that he sure had me beat in teaching him something. I was alright when it come to starting a colt and taking the rough off him, but after that I sure had to take a back seat from Flint.

The boys was rounding up fresh horses and the wagons was getting ready to pull out again, all the corrals was being used and every rider was topping off the horses cut to him; from ten to fifteen head of the big fat geldings is what made a "string," and the company saw that each cowboy had all he needed far as horse-flesh was concerned.

And when the four and six horse teams was hooked on the "chuck," "bed," and "wood" wagons and the big corral gates was opened to let the remuda follow, every cowboy was on hand and ready. "The pilot" (rider piloting the wagon through the roadless plains and breaks) started, the cook straightened out his team and followed with the chuck wagon, then the "flunky" next with the bed wagon, and the "nighthawk" (night herder for the saddle-horses) on the wood wagon took up the swing, then last came the day wrangler bringing up the rear with upward of two hundred head of saddle stock, the remuda.

Fifteen or more of us riders rode along the side, doing nothing in perticular but keeping our ponies right side up till we come to the country where the work begins. The whole outfit moved on a fast trot and sometimes going down a sag you could see the cook letting his team hit out on a high lope, and the rest was more than aching to keep up.

Two more such outfits was to start out soon for other directions and on other ranges. I went along with the first; the broncs I'd just started a few weeks before was in the remuda and on the trail of eddication to the ways of the critter, the same as the bunch I'd took along early that spring.

In this new string of broncs I was putting through the ropes, there was another special little horse what promised to come up along with Brown Jug as a cowhorse. But I was kinda worried, he was *too* good, never bucked once and seemed to try too hard to learn. His kind of a horse was hard for me to make out, 'cause they was few. I always felt they was waiting for a chance to get you, and get you good whenever that chance showed up.

I figgered a horse with a good working set of brains like he had ought to've done *something*, but all he did do was to watch me like a hawk in every move I'd make; and he was so quiet when I was around that I naturally felt kind of nervous, thinking he might explode and tear up the scenery 'most any minute.

But he stayed good and kept a-learning fast, and even though I figgered he might be one example of a horse in a thousand, I was still dubious when I turned him and a few others of my broncs over to the boys. I wished he'd bucked, once anyway.

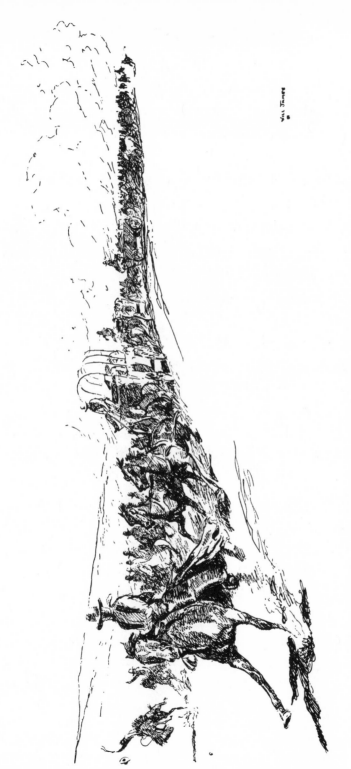

Two more such outfits was to start out soon for other directions and on other ranges.

I kept my eye on him, and every time it was his turn to be rode I was always surprised to see how docile he was. The new hand what was riding him made an awful fuss over "Sundown," as he'd called him (he was too much of a puzzle for *me* to name) and the two was getting along better than I ever expected.

With Brown Jug, he was showing a little orneriness now and again, but that was to be expected, and Flint could 'most always talk him out of it. He done the work though, and was getting so he could turn a "bunch-quitting" critter so fast she'd think she was born that way.

And, if you'd asked me right quick which one of them two ponies, Brown Jug or Sundown, would make the best cow-horse I'd said Brown Jug; on the other hand, if you'd let me think it over for a spell it'd been that to my way of thinking that the two horses don't compare; they're both working fine, but I trust Brown Jug and I can't as yet trust Sundown. Anyway, to put myself in the clear I'd said "let's wait and see."

My broncs being all took away but four, a string of "cut," "circle," and "night" horses are turned over to me and I gets in on circle day-herd and night-guard with the rest of the boys, so now I can watch the colts I'd started get their finished eddication.

Fall was coming on and the air was getting crimpy; the light frosts was turning the grass to brown, and the old ponies was developing a hump in their backs and had to have their bucking space to warm up in before straightening out and tending to business.

For the good old honest hard-working cow-horse does buck, and buck mighty hard sometimes, specially on cold mornings, but he's never "scratched" for it. The cowboy a-setting atop of him will only grin at the perticular way the pony has of unlimbering for the work what's ahead of him on the "cutting grounds." He'll be talked to a lot and kidded along for his "crooked ways," while he's tearing up the earth and trying to be serious in his bucking, and never will either the quirt or the spur touch that pony's hide while he's acting on that way, for him being a cow-horse and at the top of the ladder in saddle stock gives him a lot of privilege.

The cow-horse I'm speaking of here is the *real one*, the same you'd find anywheres, some years ago, even to-day on the big cow outfits to the east of the Rockies and on the plateaus stretching from Mexico to Canada. This cow-horse done nothing but cow work where it'd need a pony of his kind. He never was rode out on circle or straight riding and never was used anywheres outside of on the cutting grounds. All the action, strength, endurance, and intelligence that pony has was called for *there*, and the horse that could do that work and do it well was worth near his weight in gold to the country.

I well remember the time, and not so long ago, when you could buy any amount of mighty good saddle-horses for from five to twenty dollars a head, well-reined horses that could turn a Sonora "yak" quicker than you could wink; and I'll leave it to any cowman what savvies them cattle that that's saying a lot. But there was something them same ponies lacked to make 'em real cow-horses; what they lacked was intelligence, knowing where to be ahead of time when the snaky critter side-winded here or there, and put 'er out of the "main herd" before she had time to double back. Them same ponies depended too much on the touch of the rein; they couldn't see themselves what they should do, and far as they'd get in saddle stock was "dayherd," "circle," or "rope horse."

Where with the real cow-horse, he's the kind what'll work *with* the man, he's got to be able to see what should be done and do it without waiting for the feel of the rein, for sometimes things are done so quick in working a herd or cutting out a critter that the human eye or hand may be too slow, and that's where the instinct of the cow-horse comes in, to pick up the slack. He's got brains enough to know what the cowboy wants done, and he goes ahead and does it.

Man is not all responsible for making the cow-horse what he is; you got to give the pony half the credit, for after all, man only shows him the work and coaches him along some, but the horse himself does that work and will take enough interest in it as to sometimes bite a hunk of rawhide and beef right off some critter's rump if that critter happens to act ornery.

You can see feelings and wisdom all over that pony as he winds in and out through the herd. He goes along with his head straight from the body, not paying no attention to any of the bellering herd around him. The cowboy leaves the reins hanging loose and then, of a sudden the horse is given a sign which is really *no sign at all*, but anyway the pony knows *somehow* that the rider has a critter located and to be cut out; and even though there may be some cattle between him and that certain critter, he has a strong hunch just which one it is; that's enough for the cow-horse to work on.

Such a horse couldn't be bought at all, and many a time I've seen two hundred dollars or more (that was a lot of money then) offered and turned down for the likes, when the other well-reined kind could be got in trade for only a saddle blanket or a box of cartridges. Yessir, you'd had to buy the whole kaboodle, cattle, horses, range, and all, in order to get the cow-horse I'm speaking of here.

And Brown Jug, he was turning out to be just that kind of a horse. That fall after his first summer of eddication with the cow, he showed strong where in a couple more years he'd be a top cow-horse, the kind what's talked about around the cow camps from the Rio Grande to the Yellowstone. Flint was always raving about him and I'd always chip in with "well, look who started him."

Sundown was coming up right along with Brown Jug, and the new hand what was riding him sure used to get into some long sizzling arguments with Flint over them two ponies, but the argument kept neck to neck, same as it did with the horses.

They was both turned out that fall together with the rest of the remuda. That winter was easy on all

135

stock, and the horses was all packing a big fat when spring broke up.

The spring horse round-up brought in near a thousand head of saddle stock, and in one of the corrals with other horses I got first glimpse of Brown Jug and Sundown. They'd been pals all winter and where one went the other followed; if one got into a scrap the other helped him and they sure made a dandy pair.

Flint'd been complaining of getting old and stiff for a week or so past, and when he seen Brown Jug acting snorty he mentioned it again, and a little stronger this time. Finally I took the hint and told him I'd top him off for him if he wanted me to. "Sure," he says, "I don't mind."

Well sir, that little horse gave me a shaking up the likes I never had before or since, and when he finally quit and I got off, I was beginning to feel old and stiff myself, but I rode him again that afternoon and took it out of him easy enough. The next day he was all right and Flint rode him away.

In another corral something was more than raising the dust and soon as I see what causes it, I don't lose no time to climb the poles and get there. Sundown had "broke in two" *at last*. The new hand was having it out with him but he had no chance. Somehow he stayed on though and when the horse quit he fell off like a rag.

All that could be got of him was buck, fight, sulk, and stampede.

After he put a couple of boys in the hospital and come damn near getting me, he was put in the "rough-string."

I takes a turn at that horse and tired as he is he sure makes it interesting, and I don't find no time to use the quirt. He finally quits again and I was mighty glad of it. He's standing with legs wide apart, fire in his eyes and puffing away like a steam-engine and when I tries to move him out of his tracks, all I gets is a couple more hard stiff jolts. He's mad clear through and I know there's no use trying to make him do anything just then.

From then on he was just as bad this spring as he was good the spring before. All that could be got of him was buck, fight, sulk, and stampede. He was no more interested in anything else, and after he put a couple of boys in the hospital and come damn near getting me, he was put in the "rough-string."

I wasn't surprised to see him turn out that way; if anything, I kind of expected it. For even though I've seen a *few* what never bucked on first setting and stayed good all the time, I always figgered there was something wrong with 'em and could never trust 'em till I knowed for sure.

I quit the outfit that year, right after the spring round-up was over, and it was a couple of years later when I rode back into that country. The spring round-up was in full swing and a herd was being "worked" a little ways from camp.

I rides over, and there was Flint and Brown Jug working *together*, and doing the prettiest job of cutting

*That little horse without man or bridle puts 'er
out of the herd, and heads 'er for the cut.*

out I ever saw. A long-legged and long-horned staggy-looking critter was being edged to the outside of the herd, and I could see that critter had no intentions of being put out of that herd, none at all.

Pretty soon an opening shows up and Brown Jug come pretty near seeing it quicker than Flint. Anyway that critter was stepped on from there and put out before she knowed it. She tries to turn back, but the little horse was right on hand at each side step, when of a sudden Brown Jug stumbles. His foot had gone down a badger hole and he come near turning over. Flint quits him, and when the little horse straightens up the bridle is off his head. All was done quicker than you could think and the critter hadn't had time to get back to the herd.

Then, Brown Jug sees 'er, and, transformed into a lightning streak, he lands on 'er; the fur is flying off that critter's rump and that little horse without man or bridle keeps on as though nothing happened and puts 'er out of the herd and heads 'er for the cut.

Nobody says anything for a spell, but the expressions means a lot. Then the foreman, who'd seen it all, kinda grins and says: "If I had a few more horses like that I wouldn't need no men."

A few days later that same foreman piles his rope on Brown Jug, leads him out, and puts his own saddle on him. That sure set me to thinking, for even the boss is not supposed to ride any horse the company furnishes you with in your string, and still wondering I looks over at Flint, who's leading out the boss's top horse and putting *his* saddle on him.

I finds out afterwards that they'd swapped, and that Flint was to get his wages raised to boot, but I could see that Flint wasn't any too happy over the trade and I says to him, "I guess you feel about the same now as I did when *I had* to turn him over to you three years ago."

"Yes," he answers, "and worse."

But even at that, we was both mighty proud that we'd helped make Brown Jug what he was, *the top cow-horse of four remudas.*

Chapter VII

THE LONGHORNS

When we speak of the longhorns in the cow country, we most generally set back some, and think back a whole lot. And thinking, we sometimes wonder if the Spaniards realized when they brought the first of them cattle over from Spain that they was responsible for the good they done in stocking up the Southwest and making it the starting of the cow country it turned out to be.

It took a couple of hundred years for them first cattle to multiply and spread out, so that the whole of California and plum across to the Gulf of Mexico was cut up by the trails them roaming herds would make. There come a time when their trails run in with the buffalo's down in Texas; they drank of the same waters and grazed on the same flats. They changed some in build to fit in with what the country called for, and came right up with the buffalo in speed and endurance.

Then come a time when the pioneers what drifted in that country started claiming 'em, and the cattle got a *burning* feeling that they wasn't as free as before. Old Maverick claimed a good many and finally decided it'd be best to put a brand on his thousands of cattle, if he wanted to keep 'em *his*. That was before "irons" had to be recorded or before there was any such a place where you could record 'em at.

The long horned, long legged critters stayed wild and mighty spooky. They couldn't afford to pack extra fat as it'd hinder 'em in their running, and outside of keeping the few people in meat and supplying the markets with rawhide, they had nothing to do but run, accumulate, and stay wild.

They done all them things in fine style — but, all too soon (as some of the old cowmen will tell you) the railroads blazed a way towards the gold fields and other glittering facts the West held out for them who wanted to come and get it.

With the folks piling in sky high and more of 'em coming steady from acrost the ocean, it wasn't long till there was use for them buckskin cattle, and other than for the rawhide they was packing. The stockman what was already there ahead of the crowd started to keep better tab of his stock and finally got to thinking so much of 'em all of a sudden, that he'd just hang high and dry any one caught stealing any of them critters.

The cattle getting more handling and care naturally got more gentle and got so in time that you could keep sight of 'em and not even have to get your horse out of a lope; but in the thick brush or rocky countries, and wherever it was so rough that the riders rode around there was big herds stayed wild, and nobody seemed to want to fool with them just then.

But it wasn't so very long till they was pecked at, and come a time when instead of them wild bunches increasing as they should they was gradually dwindling down to a few. Them few was making themselves mighty hard to find though, and kept a-making such a good job of hiding away in their rough countries that they held their little bunches to near normal in size.

Only a half dozen years ago you could still run across a few of them wild ones right along with the wild horses, but there wasn't much if any of the old longhorn strain in 'em, for as the gentler range cattle down in the flats below was getting of the better breed and as some of them yearlings and two-year-olds was straying away and joining the wild bunch now and again, them strays would gradually kill the old strain and keep the wild ones up in breed.

But their wild instinct stayed the same, or if anything they got wilder and wiser, and I wouldn't be surprised if I was to ride along and still find a few of them wild unbranded critters even to-day. 'Cause the country they'd pick on to run in then hasn't changed much, if any, since, and as I've already said it was well

*I'd take my rope down and try my luck but that critter
would leave me as though I was standing still.*

out of the way of riders and no place to run high priced
range cattle in.

Them wild ones scattered along up through the
Rockies into the Northern States. And wherever you
could find deer, elk, and mountain lions in the cow
country was where you'd also find them wild "orejanas,"
but they was even harder to get a sight of than any
deer. They'd always see you first and had the sage
chicken beat when it come to hiding, they'd stand still
as a petrified tree and let you ride past within a few
yards of 'em if they thought they was well enough hid.
But if there was no hiding place handy they'd take to

running, and I never yet seen a horse that could catch up with 'em in their brushy, rocky territory.

I've seen 'em sometimes a little out in the open and where I thought I had a good running chance at 'em. I'd take my rope down and try my luck but that critter would leave me as though I was standing still, and hit out for the best goat country you ever saw, hardly ever breaking out of a long trot, the likes of which would sure make any mountain raised horse use all the fastest gaits he had, but there was no catching up to within roping distance of 'em.

Amongst them wild bunches you'd sometimes find near pure bred Herefords and Durhams what had turned wild from not getting enough handling or being missed out of the round-up for a couple of years, others had been let go when they was wanting to fight some rider what tried to turn 'em too quick, and that rider being too busy at the time to take the orneriness out of one of 'em just left her behind, or whichever way she wanted to go.

With the result that (like some humans) that critter thought she had somebody buffaloed for sure, and head high, pacing pretty, hits out for the tall, rough, and uncut to join the rest of the wild bunch.

Then, yearlings and two-year-olds would stray away, run across the outlaws, and follow 'em along the high steep trails. They'd get numerous, and there'd come a time when us riders would have to pack 30-30's and get 'em the best way we could till the hills was clean of 'em. They'd be hauled to the railroad in wagons, and with a bullet hole back of their ears.

In the Southern States like Texas, New Mexico, and Arizona was where the wild stuff stayed wild the longest. They had bigger and rougher scopes of country to run in than could be found further north, and they wasn't affected much by the upbreeding of the tamer herds. The reason was that for every one well bred critter what strayed away and joined 'em, there'd be two long horned "Sonora Reds" butting in and keeping up the old strain.

Them wise hombres would feed in the open from sundown till sun-up, tank up on water while it was still dark, and then hide in the thick brush all day long, never coming out till the sun went down again. Solid stockade traps was built now and again, and big hunks of salt was used for the bait, and after letting things lay quiet for a week or a month, or till the critters got over being suspicious and came regular to get their lick of the salt, a drive was made with the idea to corral the bunch just when they'd least expect it.

A few, mighty few, would be corralled in and the rest would make a snorting getaway, them few that'd get caught would also get away sooner or later, for the corral couldn't hold up against them stout necks very long, and they had a way of working with them horns of theirs that would tear up 'most anything.

The stockmen kept a-worrying and thinking of new ways to handle them outlaws and tame 'em down so they could be run with the herd-broke range cattle. Shooting 'em was a waste of meat and hauling 'em in to the local butcher shop didn't bring a satisfactory price, besides there was times when them same butcher shops would have more beef than they could sell, and shipping took longer than the meat could wait to be still good.

And what was worse yet, was that a lot of young stock strayed away and joined them wild bunches every year, and the stockman saw where he sure had to do something about it — so, worrying along on that subject a new scheme was hatched out, a scheme that might seem kind of cruel to folks what never had any dealings with range stuff, but I'm sure that with a little experience along that line, them same folks would agree that even if it was a little cruel, it was also *mighty necessary.*

Part of that scheme was, that after each cowboy had picked two ropes, one being tied on the back of the saddle for emergency, and mounted on the best rope-horse the outfit could hand 'em, they'd line out, about twenty riders of the kind what savvied how to handle the whale-line in the thick brush.

Like one time when a big circle was made. I was with the bunch and by the cracking of the brush ahead once in a while we could tell that a few of the critters was stirred up and getting together. Our intentions was

151

to keep 'em going straight but the snaky critters was leery of openings; they stuck along to where the brush was the thickest and we'd have to lean away down alongside our horse's neck to keep from getting pulled off by the thick branches. Even at that there was places them daggone cattle went through on a high lope and where a lone horse couldn't follow on a walk and we had to go around. All that time them wild ones kept on the run, and we sure had to do some tall travelling to keep track of their whereabouts.

We didn't have a chance to crowd 'em, but we kept manoeuvring around and riding till we had 'em near the little openings and then — things started to happen and we prepare for action. Not worrying about what limbs and stickers could do to our faces and hands we spur on full speed ahead, each cowboy with his hat pulled down hard a-squinting through his horse's ears and packing a "hungry loop." We form a circle around the "orejanas" (unbranded cattle) before they know what's what and we've got 'em jammed in a small opening — but from all indications they don't figger on us holding 'em there — and we don't, not no more than a second, but in that second we have enough time to each pick our victim.

They break through and by us in all directions, loops are spread out and circle around big longhorns, the slack is pulled up, and the steers are going one way while the ponies are going another. There's an awful commotion and mixture of dust, ropes, steers, ponies, and men. Hollering and laughing cowboys, bellering mad critters, and cracking branches all throwed in.

The critter that come my way and I tied onto was good enough to hit the end of the rope fast and wicked and bust hisself into a fine laying position. I takes advantage of it and ties him down right there, and quicker than you could wink I shakes down my other rope and prepares for another victim, sees one what's trying to get out of the entanglements and snares it. About that time, I feels myself going up about ten feet, makes a circle in the air, and come down in a catclaw bush; I gets a glimpse of my horse where he'd come down flat on his back, and then I see the cause of the whole upheaval making his getaway.

It was a big spotted bull, the kind what wouldn't let a small object like a horse and a man keep him from going straight ahead to where he was headed, and I happened to be in his way. But he don't get to go far even at that. Two ropes pile in on him at once from two other riders, one of them ropes snaps like a thread and sings by like a bullet, but it checked him some till another rope was layed in the place of it, and it wasn't long till he was stretched out like any common critter.

In the meantime my little horse had picked himself up and was holding his own against the critter I'd caught, and that critter outweighed him a good hundred pounds; my saddle was slipping and I scrambles out of the scratching catclaw bush just in time to pull 'er straight, gives the steer some slack, and then goes the

It was a big spotted bull, the kind what wouldn't let a small object like a horse and a man keep him from going straight ahead to where he was headed, and I happened to be in his way.

other way, laying that critter down and tying 'er in good time.

The dust settles some and I glances over the little half a mile opening. I can only see about half of the boys who are tying down what they caught, and scattered along in the opening is somewheres around fifteen head of tied critters, but I can still hear the brush a-cracking, and, wondering if I can be of any help, rides into the thick of it.

A mile away is another and smaller opening, and there was the rest of the boys with more tied critters. The cow foreman was rolling a smoke and acted real satisfied with the catch we'd made; a little bit of a bow-legged hombre from Texas had went and broke the record by catching and tying three of the wild ones all about a mile apart, but none of us had done bad, for out of the twenty riders was twenty-four caught orejanas.

The foreman was sharpening his knife, the while remarking that a few more runs like this one would soon clean the range of the wild stuff. And when the operation is performed on them critters we'd caught and we leaves 'em free, it sure didn't take 'em long for 'em to reach the brush line again. But there they'd stop and mighty quick, turn around, and paw the earth; something had gone wrong, and somehow or other they'd took a dislike to that thick brush where they used to hide and run so well. They tried to make cover a few times while we rode by headed back for camp, but each time they'd have to turn back and wild-eyed stare at us till we got out of sight.

"It might be a few days before they can work their way out and on the big flat with the other cattle" the boss remarked as we rode on, "but they'll be there to get their water, and once they're out of this brush all the cowboys in the world couldn't drive 'em back in."

Sure enough, in a few days they was out of the brush and mixing along with the other range stuff. They'd lost all hankering for anything but the big open flats, and even though they was wild as ever we had 'em where they'd soon tame down.

We made a few more runs and finally cleaned that range of all the wild stuff, putting 'em where they'd have to be good and to stay. The hardest part was catching 'em; after that it was easy, all we did was to cut their eyelids so they couldn't close their eyes.

Them eyelids being took from 'em and leaving their eyes unprotected not only made 'em lose their liking for the thick brush, but it also took the fight out of 'em, for in both places them same eyelids are mighty necessary if the critter wants to keep her eyesight; a twig don't feel good scraping along on a bare eye, and them critters knowed that without experimenting on it and kept out of trouble in that way. They picked up on fat and gradually lost their wild ideas and speed, and it wasn't long till they was just as contented in the big flats as they was in the brush where we'd got 'em out of.

When Old Mexico turned all upside down some years ago on account of the "paisanos" wanting more beans and maybe a little land of their own, the range there was well stocked up and full of the long horned cattle, and that country being on a rampage them cattle got to belonging to any of the Mexicanos or Yaquis who could by force and with saddle horses drive 'em off for keeps or to sell. But some of the "majordomos" got wise in time and beat the thieves to it by rounding up the stock fast as they could, and taking 'em across the line in the U. S., where they was sold to American cattle buyers, who turned 'em over to the cow outfits and scattered 'em all through the range countries plum up to Canada.

I well remember one year in the spring, when some of them long horned Mexico stuff was shipped north and turned loose in the river breaks and bad lands up there. There was about ten thousand head of 'em; when we unloaded 'em at the railroad they was mighty weak and mostly all head and horns from the suffering they'd went through in the country they'd just left.

They was trailed for a few hundred miles and turned loose amongst the gumbo and many-colored pinnacles, but there was feed a-plenty and the six months them cattle ranged in there sure made 'em hard to recognize both in looks and action. They hadn't seen a human in all that time and when I say they was wild just puts it kind of mild to what they really was.

When time come to round 'em up that fall, us boys was glad to find that there'd be very few drags in them, if any, and there wasn't. We'd ride the top of the ridges, let out a war whoop, fire a few shots from our six-shooters and them steers wasn't slow getting down into the draws. You could near hear their tails a-popping as they'd slide off the side of a pinnacle, and all you could tell of their whereabouts was the dust cloud they'd stir up. A few of the wildest went so far as to run theirselves down, get overheated with the big fat they was packing, and never cool off till they was stiff and dead.

There maybe was no rider to within a mile of 'em, but once they'd get kettled and stampede away they never knowed when to stop and they'd still be going at full speed when the death cold would overtake 'em and leave 'em flat to earth, never to run no more.

But the average of them cattle was mighty nice to handle; there was no slow poky riding when they was around, and if you knowed their ways everything was hunkydory; if you didn't you'd most likely find yourself doing a lot of wild riding without result only maybe wear your horse out. Some of the bunches we'd round up would be so wild that even while holding the herd on the cutting grounds, they'd keep on milling around and keep up a high lope. No man would ride inside of that herd unless he wanted 'em to just fly away like a bunch of quail. The cutting out was done from the outside of the herd, and when a steer was wanted out, the rider would just chip in on him, separating him from the rest of the herd before he knowed it.

He'd come out of the edge like a cannon ball, and the cowboy closest to him would sure have to do some tall riding to keep that steer from hitting for the hills

That ornery critter will find his head brought up right alongside his hind quarters.

instead of for the "cut" where he was wanted. There was times when the steer would get spooky and mad, and wouldn't turn even if you'd fan him acrost the face with your rope, sometimes that fanning would get him on the "prod" (fighting mad) and then them long horns of his would get mighty dangerous to both man and horse, but the *cowboy* never lets a critter get away, he'll take his rope down, shake out a loop and dab it on around that six-foot spread of horns as the steer rushes in on him, misses (sometimes) and on past. The steer turns and makes another grand rush, and the cowboy will stay ahead out of his reach letting the slack of his rope drag on the ground. And when that same steer steps over the whale-line dragging along under him is when something happens, which sure upsets his plans of attack and everything in general.

The cowhorse'll pick up speed, the rope'll tighten up, and of a sudden that ornery critter will find his head brought up right alongside his hind quarters, lifted up in the air a few feet, only to be jerked down again, and not at all gently. The wind is knocked out of him sudden, and he's tied down with the "piggin string" before he can get it back.

The cowboy might leave him lay there to cool off for a spell and ride back to the herd, coiling up his rope on the way. When that steer is let up again he's most generally dubious about starting another fight and will most likely lope back to the cut kind of peaceable.

The first few that are cut out from the main herd for that "cut" sometimes couldn't
be held in one spot, and they would have to be roped and tied down.

In starting a cut with them kind of cattle, the first few that are cut out from the main herd for that "cut" (as we call the bunch separated out) sometimes couldn't be held in one spot, and they would have to be roped and tied down; we'd keep on a-tying 'em down till there was enough there to keep the others we'd still be cutting out from getting too frisky or lonesome. Them what was tied down was a kind of an attraction for the others that was foot-loose and they'd stick around taking a sniff at the tied critters till there was enough of a herd cut out with 'em to keep 'em all company. After that, they was easy enough to hold till the herd was worked.

I'm sorry to say for the cowboy that there ain't no more of them cattle left, that is, not enough of 'em to speak of. The few you'll find are in the movies or following the rodeos, where the contestants ride and rope 'em both, then there might be a few more running loose on the range or up in the hills and turned wild again, but you might just as well say that they're gone, and gone for good. For with the limit of the range there is nowadays there's got to be cattle on it that'll bring the most value per head, and I can't say that the longhorn was ever much of a beef producer, not comparing with the mixed Hereford and Durham stock you'll find on the range now.

And when I say I'm sorry for the cowboy that there's no more of the longhorn, it's that I know how much the cowboy liked to work them cattle. I know how nice they was to stretch a new rope on, and how hard one of them steers would hit the other end, take all the kinks out of it and make 'er sing the whole forty-foot length.

Yessir, and them cattle was a lot of company too and always up to something. If they'd stampede they always done a good interesting job of it and make us ride for all we was worth and then some, and even when the nights was still and quiet they'd make you wish you could see through the dark so you could tell what they'd be up to then.

Like, for instance, the whole herd may be bedded down and resting contented like, two or three of us boys would be riding around 'em steady, keeping our distances apart and singing to 'em as we'd ride and all would seem hunkydory, but there was always a few of them natural born leaders in each herd, the kind that never sleeps much, and them would sure have to be watched mighty close. They'd wait till the riders made the round and was far enough away so they could make a sneak without being heard; then they'd ease out and step light till they was far enough and safe to break into a run and make their getaway.

But us boys was on night guard for the purpose of keeping 'em all together, and that we tried to do with the result that not many could ever sneak out without we caught up with 'em and turned 'em back in the herd.

You couldn't very well go to sleep on the job when them cattle was around, and whether it be on day herd, night guard, or on circle they had a way about 'em that sure kept a cowboy close to his saddle. There was plenty of times when them critters would get over-ornery and when the cowboy would cuss 'em for a brainless animal, but there was things would happen every day while riding amongst 'em what would make the cowboy think again, and he'd wind up to admiring 'em and wondering how they could be so wise and in so many ways.

I remember how down in the border States where the water-holes are miles from the feed, the cattle would string out every two or three days and head for the troughs eight to twelve miles up into the foothills; there'd be a rocky trail most of the way over and too long for the little calves to make, so they'd be left behind.

Instinct, or maybe brains, made them little week-old fellers find a hiding spot before their mammies left for the day trip to water. They'd cuddle up under any kind of brush where they'd be hid best and go to sleep till their mammies came back. Many a time I've rode in on 'em when they was hiding that way, but they wouldn't move and you couldn't see 'em unless your horse near stepped on 'em. If they did have to move they wasn't at all slow about it and for a distance would sure make themselves hard to catch; they'd travel along at full speed, make a circle, and if by that time you was gone would come right back, lay down, and hide at the exact spot where their mammy'd left 'em.

Amongst 'em would be a full-grown, long, and lanky steer with horns of the kind that could more than meet an argument with most anything.

I've seen times when there'd be half a dozen or more of them little calves left behind that way and all hid along within a few feet of one another. One of them would maybe get out of his hiding place to stretch for a while, then up would come another one till they was all out and a-stretching, then of a sudden you'd hear a little beller out of one of 'em and tail up, kicking and a-bucking, he would race out across the flat, make his little circle, and come back. The rest of 'em would take up his lead and perform the same and play on that way till all the stiffness from the hiding position they'd been in was gone, when they'd hide again and wait for their mammies to relieve 'em.

But what always used to set me to thinking the most, was when I'd come across a bunch of them little fellers laying around anywheres, and not at all hid. The reason they wasn't hiding just then was a good one, for right amongst 'em would be a full-grown, long, and lanky steer with horns of the kind that could more than meet an argument with 'most anything.

That steer would stay on the job as guardian till the mothers trailed back. Along about sundown you could see 'em; picking up speed and walking faster and faster, they'd start bellering for their calves a mile away and the closer they'd get, the more they'd beller and the faster they'd walk, till they'd finally break into a trot, and tired as they'd be from that long trip, besides packing all the water they could hold, they'd manage to leave the "dry stuff" behind and get to their calves quick as they could.

The little fellers, hearing their mammies coming, begin to perk up their ears, then break out on a run to meet 'em, and even though to the human eye they may all look alike there's no confusion with the cow and her calf about which belongs to which. The nursing goes on and all seem plum satisfied with everything in general, the big steer finds himself all alone and, after watching the proceedings for a spell, seeing that all is O K, trails out by his lonesome, headed for the water-hole miles and miles away.

If a lone cow was making a losing fight trying to protect her calf, all she had to do was let out a call and there'd be a herd of big steers answering it.

So there you be, while that critter had no use for the human and wasn't at all affectionate in any way, not mentioning how contrary and ornery she'd get or how sometimes she'd make you travel to keep out of her horns' way, there was occasions a-plenty when you'd find yourself a-cussing at 'er orneriness and at the same time admiring the wise way that critter did have of being ornery and keeping you a-guessing.

And what's to their credit is, if trouble come they'd meet that trouble together and fight it *together* to a finish.

If a lone cow was making a losing fight trying to protect her calf, all she had to do was let out a call and there'd be a herd of big steers answering it; and whatever the enemy was, bears or wolves, they was put on the run and making far apart tracks. The human is the only enemy they had that would make 'em scatter and keep 'em a-dodging, and they took it out on him in ways that was ornery, sometimes even getting the best of him too.

Chapter VIII

PIÑON AND THE WILD ONES

Years ago, when horses wasn't worth keeping tab on and even their hide wouldn't bring a dollar, the range stuff — studs, mares, colts — ran most all unbranded. Broke stock was kept, but they wasn't worth much either, far as money was concerned. They strayed everywhere and picked their own range, winter or summer. Once in a while some Indian would catch a fresh horse to break for his own use. Outside of that, the range horses wasn't bothered much, if any. They got wild — wild as antelopes. What was left of the mustang strain that was running free was picked up again in the better-blooded wild horse and scattered from Sonora, Mexico, through the Buckskin Mountains in northern Arizona and up into the Nevada deserts.

There was a time when you could count them by hundreds, and it would seem as if the whole side of a mountain was moving, so covered was it with "broomtails" and so regular was they moving. Sometimes they'd get started by some rider and bunch up that way till there'd be four or five hundred in the herd. There are big valleys in the wild-horse countries — some a couple of hundred miles long and fifteen or so wide, going north and south, and flanked on both sides with steep, rough juniper and piñon-covered hills. These valleys used to be dotted with bunches of fuzztails, or wild horses.

Considered worthless at that time, they enjoyed their freedom for years until the migration of the farmer to the West started a demand for horses. In the East, too, a market sprang up, with the result that the boys around the cow camps started buying whale line. The rope was used in forty-foot lengths, with one end slipped through the fork of the saddle and tied fast to the horn, the other end swinging a twelve-foot loop.

The fuzztails was easy enough caught at first. They could be hazed into almost any kind of trap. But unless you were satisfied with some old mare or jug-headed yearling, you had to be mounted for roping a good one. Besides, roping was too slow. Generally you had to use relays of fresh horses and it was mighty hard on good saddle stock. Then the blind trap was brought into the game, and that's where Mister Wild Horse started using judgment. A trap was made either of cottonwood poles or of woven wire averaging eight feet high and fixed up with junipers to look as if it wasn't there. There was two corrals and wings stretching out sometimes a mile long on both sides of the main gate. It'd take a month or so for six of us to build such a trap, but when it was done it'd fool any human.

I remember that occasionally strangers going through the hills would get caught in our traps while following a trail and didn't know it till they were right up against the corral gate. I used often to think it'd be a humdinger of a place to run a horse thief into; he'd sure have to hoof it from there on, 'cause no horse could go through it.

The wild horses were thinning down in numbers and they were getting so they wouldn't run at every small scare. They began to save their legs and hoofs for a pinch. I remember when they would run thirty miles at just seeing some rider, not interested in ponies at all, passing through the valley. They got over running without reason and made sure that a rider was after them and meant business before they'd start. Even then they'd only keep a safe distance ahead; if the rider stopped or turned they'd gradually do the same and go on feeding.

They grew wiser right along to the ways of the human. They kept shy of the timbered hills where traps were known to be and grazed in the valleys where they could see ahead what they were running into in case running was necessary. We went to relaying on them on the flats and once in a while we'd get a bunch to work the way we wanted and head them into the hills.

If we crowded them too much they'd split and go in all directions. We had to use our heads, 'cause the fuzztail sure used his. They had no rest in the valleys or mountains. They'd leave their home range to go to another only to get chased back.

Every cow-puncher with a string of his own ponies was soon running mustangs, cow-punching being too slow. Some were good at it and others only educated the mustang and made him harder to catch. A trap with a spring and a rope buried was invented for use on trails. When it was set off the rope'd fly up, circle a leg, and draw tight. The other end of the rope was fastened to a log. A trapped mustang would tear up the scenery a heap at first and then settle down to dragging that log far as he could, leaving a trail easily followed and seldom more than four miles or so in length. This sort of trap caught some horses, but generally they were old mares, the leaders of the bunch. The fuzztail got wise to this snare and as there were cattle on the same range he'd use them as leaders. He'd follow the cattle as they started to water. If a trap caught anything, it was usually a steer that dragged the log. The leading horse would look back and nicker, seeing if her foals were all present and accounted for. And they would be.

Once while looking over the prospects for a new trap site, my outfit had stirred up a bunch of wild ones here and there to see which way they'd run. There must have been about three hundred head a few miles in front of us, covering the country at a stiff trot. We lagged behind and watched where they would naturally run without crowding.

More than two-thirds of them went through a big gap called Devil's Gate — a dandy natural place for a blind trap. We set to work there and the trap was up and strong in record time. Our saddle stock had a good rest and a steady feed of grain and they were rearing to go. The mere sight of a bunch of wild ones made them walk on two legs.

Meanwhile I'd been noticing a paint stud up on top of a big ridge at one side of the gap. He must have been a young one, 'cause there were only two fillies in his bunch. He had made his appearance a few times while we were building the trap and seemed to take a lot of interest watching us. I figured him to weigh close to eleven hundred. He was so good to look at that we decided to run him in first chance we got.

We were up long before daybreak the morning of the first run to our new trap. We'd had breakfast, our horses were caught and grain-fed, and we were riding out of camp by sun-up. It was fifteen miles to the trap and we planned to scatter from camp, hazing in wild ones on the way over. With another rider I headed on straight for the trap. We took our places close to the wings to help crowd the mustangs in and to keep them from leaving the trail before they got there — a ticklish job. We were off our horses and hidden behind a knoll, one man on each wing.

Somehow when I think of it now, I certainly feel sorry for the man that has never run mustangs. Anybody who likes excitement of the right kind sure would get it to his heart's content when looking back over the trail, winding around peaks on the mountain tops, while for two miles in depth, one right behind the other, come the wild ones, every one of them on the trail and every color of horseflesh you could think of! And all a-coming in, to order! I don't know how many heartbeats I lost or gained. And I was afraid those mustangs would hear the thumping under my shirt, for the leaders passed on the trail a few yards from where I was hid. The rest followed, sniffing for a suspicious sign; but we had taken good care that there would be none. The drags went past and I got on my horse, falling in behind. The boys caught up with us and before the mustangs knew it they was free no longer. That fence, which they couldn't see, was hard on them and skinned up quite a few, but they gradually quit hitting and started to milling. There was fifty-six head in the bunch, but scattered out as they was on the trail they seemed three times that many to anybody not used to the game.

About this time we saw the paint stud up on his ridge looking down at us. We'd get him next day, we agreed. But next day he wasn't to be seen in the neighborhood, nor the day after that. So we took our catch out of the trap by roping each one and tying one front foot to the tail close enough so he couldn't use it except to rest. They were fence-broken by this time and

For two miles in depth, one right behind the other, come the wild ones.

we took them to a big pasture furnished us by the outfit we were running for. The outfit owners wanted the range cleared of wild horses so that grazing for their cattle would be better. We was working under contract, the arrangement being that we take away all the horses caught except the branded ones. There was only one out of twenty bearing an iron and the rest we shipped or sold to buyers. It looks like easy money, but a lot of mustang-runners got disappointed in it and left the country with nothing but a few stove-up saddle horses.

The second drive to our promising trap looked better than the first. Being out on circle with three of the boys I could see that the wild ponies was coming in and taking to the trail fine. It wasn't just luck for us. It was because we'd been at it a lot and knew what we was about. We credited the mustang with brains and used ours against his. And ours won — sometimes.

The boys on the mountain flanks were riding in a steady lope with the fuzztails hitting it up half a mile or so ahead. All was working pretty and I'd already picked as a saddle horse a bald-faced, stocking-legged sorrel stud up in the lead bunch. They were as good as caught, for a quarter of a mile ahead was the wings. Then on that ridge at the right of the gap I see the familiar paint stud, appearing all excited. Head and tail up, he's coming down and heading for our bunch, snorting at every jump.

One of the boys at the wing tries to turn him back, but there wasn't a chance. That paint knows just where he's headed and what to do, and nothing but a trap fence could stop him. A loop spreads and reaches out, but it falls a couple of feet short. With a whistle and a snort the paint keeps on straight for the leaders that were behaving so well. As he nears them there's a sort of confab in horse language. And the paint takes the lead, seventy head of ponies following him! They broke out on their top speed, their tails a-popping; and down the mountain off the trail they went.

I'd figured something was going to bust when I saw the paint butting in that way and I headed my horse for the left flank of the herd. There was three of us trying to check the stampede and, even though we knew there was no use, we certainly rode and tried. We got there ahead of the paint, now running straight for us with the rest of the herd right in his dust. With our ropes over our heads we tried to faze them by yelling and whooping, but they kept coming and split on all sides of us. Two ropes sang out and settled over the paint's head with him going downhill full speed. The whale-lines stretched out like a fence, tons of horseflesh hitting them, two pounds to the ounce. It was against our judgment, but we were mad. My saddle was jerked off my horse and I went sailing with it to Mother Earth, where I saw more horses' legs at one sitting, so to speak, than ever before in my life. The other rope broke and away goes the paint, bucking down the pinnacle and dragging my saddle and another piece of rope along with him. The horse I was riding joined the wild bunch, too, and when I calculated my losses I was short a new rope, a sixty-dollar saddle, a horse, and even my six-shooter, which had taken a squatter's right in some badger hole; anyhow, I couldn't find it. We had many reasons to get the paint now. He'd turn every bunch we'd bring. He knew where the trap was and he'd give us away every chance he got.

I rode to camp back of one of the boys and the next morning I made as a substitute saddle a relay

My saddle was jerked off my horse and I went sailing with it to Mother Earth.

rigging consisting of two stirrups, a strap, and a blanket. It took thirty-five pounds' weight off my horse. We were all riding our tops that morning and I knew if we got sight of Mister Paint he was a gone gosling.

From a summit we sighted out on the flat. I took first turn and sashayed him for a good fifteen miles. Then one of the boys relieved me and took him on. When I saw the paint again, the fourth man was at him; he'd covered a good sixty miles in mighty fast time. I could see he was going on his nerve, but he had plenty of it. The fifth man jumped him, and after a quarter-mile run on a fresh horse the paint was his. There was no trace of my saddle with him; my rope must have broken at the

I took first turn and sashayed him for a good fifteen miles.

hondoo. An unravelled piece of the other rope still hung to his neck.

We sure took good care of that boy so he wouldn't get away. We put him in the trap he'd watched us build, leaving him there overnight to think things over. In the morning we found him stretched out with a broken neck. He had hit the corral a little too hard.

Everything went well during the next circle we made till we got to that spot where the paint had spoiled things. It seemed as if there were a couple of fuzztails from the first bunch that remembered the turning point. Two of them took the lead away from our trap, at any rate, and we lost the bunch. It got us on edge to see such a promising trap site turn out so disappointing.

We ran two weeks and had caught forty head more when one day lightning struck and burnt a juniper down right in the main gate. That cooked our goose. You couldn't get a mustang within a mile of it.

Figuring on working both sides of it without having to turn a bunch, we gave our next trap two main gates. We caught some thirty-odd head in the first run. On the second day we lost all we brought in, the bunch turning within a few yards of the gate. The trouble was that a few doggone dudes from town had come up hunting sage chickens, which they cooked on a brush fire within a few steps of the trail. They must have been eating as they walked, for there were chicken bones chewed up and scattered all along. Their Number Ten shoe-prints were easily visible, and you couldn't push a mustang through there with a snow plough. We closed that gate and started running in from the other side. The jinx was on us there, again; a few head of stock had died a half mile up the draw above the trail and a sniff was enough to turn off the suspicious mustangs, for when they're being chased that way they are always suspicious. Mustangs may even be superstitious; many a time I've seen crows, flying over the leaders, squawk them off the trail. I've had them turn on me for no reason that I could see. But that's where they've got it on us humans; their instinct, sense of smell and vision are developed to the hair-trigger point. It's plain wild-horse sense.

We built two more traps and changed our tactics each time. Even with our bad luck we caught more horses than anybody else in that country. The boys I was with was professional horse hunters — best hands at it I ever saw. And I was no slouch myself or they wouldn't have had me with them. Our main idea was to let the mustangs think they was getting away. For instance, if we wanted them up on the mountain or wherever our trap was, we'd make a bluff to run them in the opposite direction and nine times out of ten they'd double back into the trail to our trap.

We'd even build rag wings three or four miles long on each side of the mountain to our trap by stringing a single wire on far-apart posts with rags dangling from it. That would turn a few, but sometimes some wise old mare in the lead would take a chance and the others would follow through.

The popular idea of wild horses usually has some beautiful stallion heading the band, but, although he may be beautiful, the stallion seldom takes the lead. I've seen the old boy many a time half a mile or so behind his bunch; he's there to see that his mares, if chased, are getting away. He doesn't want to leave any behind and will even nip some of the drags to make them run faster and keep up with the rest. Going to water or following a trail some old mare is always ahead with her foals following. The only time the stallion may take the lead is when the herd is in a pinch and crowded. But even then he'll circle around his mares, keeping them together and looking for the best way out at the same time. He'll find it if there is any. When two bunches meet, the stallion in each goes ahead by himself and has a little conversation with the other. The mares and colts wait and graze till the discussion is over and the stallion returns. Then the trail is resumed unless that talk winds up in a fight. Often it does — the winner taking all and the loser hits out alone. When the loser comes across another band it's another scrap, and if he wins, the bunch is his, whether they want him or not. Should some mare get ornery and want to leave, that stallion puts his head down, shoots his ears back, and, looking wicked, hazes her back to the herd.

We caught a lone stud once that had been whipped out of some bunch — caught him when he thought he was getting away from us. There were no other horses in the trap and he felt mighty spooky. A few of us was sitting on our horses at the main gate waiting till one of the boys went round and opened the little corral to drive him in. He'd been circling around testing the trap here and there and had found it mighty solid. He knew his only way out was the way he came in. He stopped and sized us up for a spell, fire in his eye. Then with ears back and teeth showing he made a bee line for one of the boys inside and off his horse. The man started to dodge out of the stud's way but he went down. As Mister Stallion, heading for his man, went past our line a loop sailed out and dropped over his neck. He was drug down to the little corral and taken to the pasture with the next bunch caught. A month later we found him dead. It wasn't lockjaw or starvation that killed him. He was fat as a seal and had plenty of feed and water. He just died of a broken heart.

The wild horse I'm speaking of here is of the bunch-grass countries, where he has a chance to develop and grow. His brain is a heap keener than the desert horse's; he's bigger and well proportioned, and on an average better built than any thoroughbred you ever saw. He's all action and steel, and if I had my pick between a thousand-dollar Arabian steed and a common fuzztail for my own use I'd rather have the one with the snort and the buck, 'cause I know the trail between suns is never too long for him, no matter how scarce the feed or water may be.

Plenty of times I've heard fellers talk of running down the wild ones with grained horses in the spring of the year, when the fuzztail is supposed to be weak. I've seen it tried and sometimes done, but I always figgered it a mighty hard proposition. Fact is, I've seldom seen the fuzztails when they was weak — not in that particular country anyhow; and unless a feller has a lot of good saddle horses to run the legs off and an income that keeps him from worrying about a living, I'd call it a mighty poor way of going at it. The wild one is always ready to go a long way, spring, summer, fall or winter; he can usually show you where the trail ends, and you'll be by your lonesome when he does it.

I remember a bunch of boys who had come up fresh from Texas, all good hands at roping and riding

*The wild horse is always ready to go a long way,
spring, summer, fall, or winter.*

and savvying stock. They was drawing wages from the
same outfit we was running horses for, and I'd come
up to their camp for a piece of beef. I stuck around for
a spell to hear news of the lower country and while we
was talking a bunch of mustangs came to water at the
creek just half a mile below camp. One of the boys sees
them and remarked: "How tame they are, coming to
water that close to camp."

"They ain't tame," I said. "They're just full of
confidence in themselves. Try your luck catching one
of 'em."

No sooner said than done. The rider snared the
fastest horse he could get and was up and at them with

his rope dragging in less time than it takes to tell it. That part of the country, by the way, was full of junipers and piñons with deep washes and high ridges. The mustangs disappeared over the ridge and Tex was right in their dust.

In about an hour he came back, his rope all coiled up neat and where it belonged. He wasn't disappointed — it was just a new one on him and he wondered how it was done.

"Sure enough," he said, "the earth just swallowed 'em. I thought they was right in front of me and when I topped the ridge I couldn't see hair nor hide of 'em. I circled and looked for tracks, but that whole country is already full of horse tracks."

Texas holds the record for good cow hands, but cow-punching and mustang-running are a heap different. I suppose this particular bunch of mustangs strung themselves out straight ahead till they got out of sight in the thick brush and then just doubled back close to their own trail. Of course Tex just kept going, and by the time he circled, the fuzztails were out of the country.

Before leaving we built two more traps on that range, with pretty fair results. All together we had caught, shipped, and sold more than five hundred head. With winter coming we decided to pull out for the south and run some more when the snow wasn't so deep.

The superintendent of the outfit rode up to our camp the day before we left and said his instructions from the owners was to kill off the rest of the mustangs, two dollars a head being offered as bounty. Of course the owners didn't know anything about running stock, but they realized from what the superintendent said that something would have to be done to save the range for the cattle. The owners was probably leading a soft life back East busy with their social functions and taking shower baths in champagne regular. I guess they didn't realize or care what they were condemning to die just so there could be more room for the cattle and a bigger income for themselves.

Naturally, we refused flat, saying that if we didn't want to, or couldn't, catch the mustangs, we sure wouldn't shoot them. And we left.

By the time we got to our next mustang territory our saddle stock was leg-weary, and after sizing up the country we decided to postpone any more running till along about spring. In the meantime we took possession of a deserted mining camp and made ourselves at home for the winter. We kept graining our horses and with the bunch grass in the hills they grew fat. Some of the boys made McCarthies, or hair ropes, while others worked with the steel traps. Pretty soon we had a good-sized bale of furs to ship — coyotes, bobcats, badgers, and one cougar that was shot. We kept down expenses, and managed to be present at all dances within sixty miles of our camp.

Towards spring we built three water traps — just a corral in plain sight built around a water hole with a smaller corral connected in which to keep what was caught, and by that keeping the main corral for another bunch. There was two main gates, one on each side, and they was left open, as we wasn't figgering on catching any mustangs just then. As water got scarce, later on — water holes being some forty miles apart — the mustangs gradually came up closer to our traps every night. Finally, one night I saw the tracks of some that had been right inside the trap to drink. They got used to it and they'd come in one gate, drink what they wanted, rub themselves for a spell, and leave through the other gate. In time there was from four to six bunches watering at each trap.

We kept away and let the mustangs run back and forth through our traps for over a month. We'd ride the whole country and at each water hole where there was no traps a man would be there to keep the wild ones from drinking. Then they'd begin to trail out for the springs we had corralled.

A day came when the flats of the desert went dry as a bone. It was our time to work. We split in pairs, two men to each trap, closed one gate and left the other open. Near the traps we had dug holes big enough for a man to get into comfortable, covering them over with poles, dirt and brush. We'd take shifts of half a night — the wild horse waters at night mostly — watching from these holes. One man slept while the other watched. I had second guard the first night and missed the fun, but the first man on guard pulled the trigger rope and caught twelve head. Counting the catches in the other traps we got twenty-seven of the wild ones that night.

The next night I had better luck. While I was in the hole familiar snorts told me that a bunch was coming. I could tell they was suspicious of man scent even though I was quite a distance from the gate. They'd come up a few steps, then go back; the lead mare would start ahead and the stud would circle around, his head up and taking in all he could see. At times he'd turn the lead mare back, but he wasn't sure. The bunch was in need of water bad. Finally, half of them went in, only to come out again, snorting at every jump and shying at nothing. I knew they'd come back, and they did after a good hour's wait. I was wondering if I could catch the whole bunch, but when they came again they seemed to get reckless and crowded in and around the water. While the stud was acting nervous around his bunch I pulled the trigger and the gate closed with a bang. The bunch stampeded at the noise and struck out for the other side of the corral, the earth shook. As they hit the wire it yielded a little and kicked them back off their feet. Those mustangs tested the whole corral — every inch of it — but it was built for that purpose. Heavy wire cables had been stretched around the top and bottom of each post, making the whole corral as if it was one piece; woven wire was attached to the cable top and bottom and wired to the posts, being allowed to hang slack for give and take. I kept away from the trap after I'd made my catch, 'cause my appearance there just then would have made the horses break their necks hitting the other side.

The southern ponies were not nearly so big or so well built as the northern horses we'd been running, and they was caught more easy, 'cause they hadn't been chased so much. Blind traps was unknown in that country. An open corral with long wings or a water trap was the average. Southern mustangs was easy turned and handled, and on a fast horse you could often ride close enough to one to pile your rope on him. They was generally caught around water holes, 'cause when full of water the mustang can't run very fast or far. But in that shape, he's easy choked if the rider don't ease up on the rope in time.

Our traps began to wear out after a while, and the mustangs, still running loose, learned to keep shy of the closed water holes. There was no escaped fuzztail to give us away, but the bunches was leaving the country and hitting for new range. We opened all the gates again and left the traps for a couple of months. A few bands of wild ones came back and started watering, but when we closed the gate on the other side, leaving only the trap gate open, they got suspicious. Their snorts was all that was necessary to let us understand that they knew the corral was ready for business, and in a long lope they hit back to the country from which they came.

Once we caught a black stud that had been caught before and was already acquainted with the nature and strength of a trap. Ours being new to him and well hid, he was fooled just long enough to be caught again but he didn't waste time hitting the sides of the trap as the rest of the bunch with him did. He figgered just how high that trap was and used the speed he was coming in with to clear it! He never checked up or stopped. He sailed right on over the top and never touched the cable. The fence at that particular place was nine feet high. A mustang seldom jumps anything; he tries to go through first. But this one had learned there was no going through. I never saw anything so pretty as when that black horse got clean away. Our mouths was wide open, and we stared. It was a well-done job too; for instead of breaking into a run after clearing the fence he just trotted off stiff-legged, covering fifteen feet to the pace. His feet seemed not to touch the ground, his muscle working and his head up, he looked back at us over his shoulder and fanned his long tail about just as if he was waving by-by to us. He stopped sudden on top a little hill three hundred yards or so from us, and facing about he gave us a farewell whistle before proceeding, full of pride, out of sight. Pete looked at me solemn and said: "My God, Bill, I'd give a good hundred for that horse!"

The hardest horse to trap is the one that has been broke to riding or work and then gets away. No matter how gentle he was when he got away, the sight of his home range and the wild ones makes him forget all that man has ever taught him. The only thing he remembers and uses is his knowledge of the ways of man. This knowledge stands him in good stead when he sees some rider fogging down on him; that wise hombre takes the lead and the bunch follows, sure that they've got a leader that knows the ropes.

I've known of mustangs getting away after being gentled that travelled two hundred miles or more, through settlements, over bridges and railroad tracks, even swimming rivers to their country of freedom. They'd feed as they travelled, not even stopping to drink; they'd go up or down a stream, dragging their noses in the water till their thirst was satisfied. If you could catch up to them before getting close to their home territory they wasn't so hard to handle; being in a strange country, they'd give up easy enough. The mustang has a good working set of brains; if he sees, for instance, that whoever is chasing him is riding a tired horse he knows it and will circle round, tail and head up, looking pretty and teasing the rider to come on.

Talking of horse sense, let me bring in a chestnut I'd picked on as a saddle horse. He needed some care for the cuts and scratches he'd got when connecting with the trap. I roped and snubbed him, put on the hackamore, and picketed him to a log in a little meadow close to the corral. He had fifty feet of soft rope to run on and the feed was good, but the flies and mosquitoes was hard on him, the deer fly and the bulldog fly doing the most tormenting; and that poor little chestnut had a lot of places open for the pests to work on. I wanted to heal up the sores before thinking of breaking him, and his badly peeled head gave me a lead to show my feelings.

The first time he saw me coming I'd thought he'd leave the country until the heavy log caught in a stump; then he bit and kicked at the picket rope, I let him have it out and kept coming closer, working round till I touched his head. He'd run his nose up along my arm, then snap at it and strike with both front feet at the same time. I worked pretty easy, 'cause I didn't want him to lose any more of that hide, and he only showed the right spirit according to his lights, even if he did come within close striking distance of my face. I could have taken advantage of him and ridden him while he was sore, when he would have been easier to break maybe, but I had a lot of time and I liked him. Before long I had his peeled head all covered with fly-proof healing salve; I smeared a lot of that salve on all the sore spots from the tip of his nose to the middle of his back. I'd do that twice and three times a day till finally he got to looking for me and nickered when he saw me coming. He'd come to meet me as far as the picket rope would let him and follow me around wherever I went. I kept smearing salve on all the cuts plumb down to his hoofs and he'd stand there just watching me, not a bit of harm in him. He was healing up fast and hair began to cover the scars. One day I even got on him bareback and rode him around the log. He took that all in as part of the healing process, I guess. Anyhow, he got over being afraid of me.

He was the kind of sensitive horse that wouldn't stand rough handling, and his ten hundred pounds of fine bone and muscle could back his sentiments in that regard. He was full of fight and only a little jerking around was needed to start him going. I didn't jerk him but kept on handling him easy, until one day I slipped my saddle on him. He did just what I expected, giving the prettiest exhibition of bucking I ever saw. I was wondering how hard a ride I'd have to put up to stick him when I saddled him again a few days later, but he fooled me. I led him round a bit; he stood quiet till I got my seat. I pulled him on one rein a couple of times and finally lined him round the corral. He just trotted on and kept looking back at me. I was expecting him to go to pieces at any minute, but nothing doing. He acted as if everything was O. K. so long as I was up there sitting on him, and after smelling the saddle a few times he figgered that that must be all right too.

That summer and fall the chestnut and I had a lot of dealings together. I was headed for no place in particular — just drifting. I had a pack horse along and on top of him was my home and grub. We'd travel for a spell and take it easy when we'd strike places where the feed was good. We was out of the wild-horse country when I quit putting hobbles on the chestnut and we was getting pretty thick by that time. Piñon, as I called him, wouldn't go more than a few hundred yards from my camp, no matter how scarce the feed was; and many a time I would wake up at night to find that he and the pack horse was bedded down right in the kitchen, you might say — just a rope's length from my bed.

Piñon was no sugar-eater or pet. He was just a fifty-fifty partner of mine. He never had a feed of grain, but once in a while I'd give him a biscuit from my small Dutch oven. He'd pack me all day long, but when I decided to camp I'd always tend to Piñon and the other horse before straightening out my camp or cooking a meal. If on a real hot day I'd come a cross a juniper in the foothills, I'd always stop in what shade there was under it and loosen up my saddle to air Piñon's back and scratch him behind the ear every once in a while.

One day I had to stop in a town to get some grub and tobacco. I left Piñon and the other pony at the stable corrals. Seeing that the big mangers was full of hay, I sneaked out when I thought Piñon wasn't looking. But he soon found out that I was missing and the little son-of-a-gun was sure making himself heard! Well, sir, I wouldn't have taken the whole world for that little horse just then, or I guess any other time, either. I finally told the stable boy to watch out that Piñon didn't hurt himself on the fence and started out toward the main street of town, walking a heap faster than I generally do. I got my stuff and came back as quickly as I could, to find a mighty restless pony waiting for me. I saw that I would simply have to camp with him that night, so I picked out a clean spot in an out-of-the-way corner of the corral to roll out my bed. Piñon was right there to see what was up; and as soon as he discovered I was making my camp, as he'd seen me do many times before, he was satisfied and walked away to eat. I figgered having lost his freedom and being in a strange country he looked to me as a sort of leader and partner; I felt that he was a little orphan and kind of needed me.

This isn't intended to be a lot of sentimental talk I'm handing you. Piñon might have been the exceptional horse in a thousand, but I find that if you make a pal of any gelding and talk to him often, treating him about as you would a dog, you'll have a stouter friend in the horse. A dog may go mad, turn on you, and chew you up if grub's scarce and he gets hungry enough; but the horse will pack you as far as he can and die doing it. If you're out on the desert and you both give out he won't howl his sufferings into your ear. As for brains and honesty — I hate to compare a dog or any other animal with the deep-hearted, long-winded pony of the Western ranges.

For years Piñon and I roamed the hills, valleys, and deserts, and gradually the time came when if I went away he wouldn't fret so much; he knew I'd surely come back, and I always did.

When the war broke out and I joined in I felt as if I had some one dependent on me; but then men was leaving their mothers, wives, and children behind. Before taking off my boots, chaps, and spurs for the uniform I saddled old Piñon and headed for a country where I knew the mustangs was free from runners and where the range was good. I was leading an extra horse to ride back. When in a few days I rode up on the pass where Piñon was to get his freedom once more I could see here and there down in the valley a few bunches of wild ones, and a couple of miles down the ridge I could make out four head feeding. A bunch so small generally is young studs kicked out of a herd by an older stallion. I knew this bunch would let Piñon come in and run with them, so I headed down in the wash and out of sight.

I'm facing the breeze now, making it possible for me to come pretty close without the wild ones getting wind of me. Within fifty yards of them, with a small ridge between us, I slip off the chestnut and sneak through the buckbush to get a peek at what sort of ponies they are. I see marks on their backs showing that they was once saddle horses, turned wild again, and wiser than ever. A better bunch to turn old Piñon with I couldn't hope for; I am sure these can never be caught — not with Piñon in the lead, anyway.

Unsaddling quick as I can, and acting as if I'm going to camp, I lead Piñon to a place where he can get sight of the other horses. Then giving him a couple of farewell pats I drop back a little. He sees the bunch and walks up to investigate. I'm down flat on the ground, but I can tell what's going on by watching my little horse; he gets acquainted, but pretty soon, as I figgered, he comes back. I lead him up again and pat him once more, and gradually, looking back at me now and again, he works over the ridge out of sight. I'm in the wash where my other horse is tied and, grabbing my chance, ride back for the summit fast as I can make it, being sure to keep out of sight while getting there. On reaching the summit I look back; one horse is apart from the others, rummaging around where I was going to camp. "Great little horse!" I say to myself, and it's all I can do to keep from going back for him. Then again I figure he's a heap better off where he is. As I watch, Piñon tops the little ridge between him and the other horses. He went to them, knowing that some day I'd come back for him.

I did come back, of course, but it was several years later. When I topped that summit once more, how good that little country, hid away from civilization, looked to me after seeing what I did of war and the suffering world! I camped in the wash close to the ridge where Piñon and I parted. Early the next morning I was up and riding the hills and valleys for a sight of him. At first I had no hopes much, but when the sun had only two hours to go in the west I saw five head a couple of miles away following the trail out of sight over a hill. I had a hunch, and, taking my chance to catch up with them, I follows.

They was on a little flat and there was no way I could come closer without being seen, so without trying to hide I tied my horse to a juniper and walked out towards them.

Piñon is in the lead, feeding. He sees me and with a snort warns the others. I talk to him just as I used to, but he's too far away, maybe, to hear me. In a big cloud of dust they're gone, but only to circle, Piñon leading them back to a safe three hundred yards from me. There he stops, tosses his head up and down, and smells the air and the ground. He's forgot me. The many days of sunlight, snow, and freedom since he saw me last have been long enough to heal many a scar and make him forget a friend. I try to get a little closer, talking away so Piñon will maybe remember. Now it almost seems that he does — he comes up a few steps as if to meet me as he used to. The other horses, doubtful of his actions, turn and start to run, which leaves Piñon alone and undecided what to do. But soon enough the wild blood wins and, with a shake of his head and his long mane to the wind, he breaks out on the easy lope I know so well, headed for the wild bunch and the freedom I had once taken away from him.

I'm always mighty proud of that little horse and I like to think of him often. There are quite a few like him in the wild-horse countries and I'm kind of sorry now so many was caught, 'cause I have a lot of respect and admiration for the mustang. The fact that he'd give us back the same medicine we'd hand him, with sometimes a little overdose, only made me feel that in him I had an opponent worthy of the game. Even though I'd get sore at them when they'd put it over on us and rub it in a little too hard, the satisfaction I'd get at catching some wise bunch didn't last very long when I'd remember that they'd be shipped, put to work, and maybe starved into being good by some hombre who was afraid of them and didn't savvy at all. For they really belong, not to man, but to that country of junipers and sage, of deep arroyos, mesas — and freedom.